Unnatural Hazard

When Inspector Angus Straun accepts an invitation to play in a Pro Celebrity golf match to mark the opening of a remote Scottish hotel he finds himself in a world that seems to have taken leave of its senses. What possible reason can there be for a complete stranger to push him out of the night express? Why should a respected antique dealer be guilty of shoplifting cannonballs? And what has prompted an elderly cleric to found a community of misfits who rule the countryside through fear? Above all, why are visitors so prone to fatal accidents on the lovely island of Sarne? Angus Straun's efforts to find out lead him to a deadly secret, long locked in the island's dark past.

BARRY CORK

Unnatural Hazard

COLLINS, 8 GRAFTON STREET, LONDON W1

William Collins Sons & Co. Ltd
London · Glasgow · Sydney · Auckland
Toronto · Johannesburg

For
Holly and Carrie

First published 1989
© Barry Cork 1989

British Library Cataloguing in Publication Data

Cork, Barry
Unnatural hazard.—(Crime Club)
I. Title
823'.914[F]

ISBN 0 00 232224 2

Photoset in Linotron Baskerville by
Rowland Phototypesetting Ltd
Bury St Edmunds, Suffolk
Printed in Great Britain by
William Collins Sons & Co. Ltd, Glasgow

CHAPTER 1

All the world wants something for nothing. You can see it at parties where the hostess has a doctor pinned in a corner while she knocks him down for some free maintenance tips on her inside at the same time as her husband is rushing an engineering student outside to ask him why the car won't start.

Policemen, particularly non-uniformed, are notoriously fair game. I know it. Everybody knows it. The trouble is that we deal with a more sophisticated public and the touch can be handled with an expertise that makes it well-nigh impossible to dodge. I fell for it at Walkers without even seeing it coming.

London has better-known salerooms than Walker's, a good firm but in no way a household word. Should you feel like spending a couple of million on a still life or getting rather more than twice as much for a Bugatti Type 41, you would do best to give the brothers Sid and Geoff a miss and settle instead for the chaps who get their sales on television. If on the other hand you're wondering where your next 'oud featherie' golf ball is coming from or you're desperate for some particular fragment of fourteenth-century horse armour, Walker's will as like as not see you through. The door to the premises in Avery Street is squeezed in between a showroom selling Rolls-Royces and the London office of a firm of Dutch solicitors, a door only recently identified by six inches of brass nameplate. After all, White's doesn't have a bloody great sign over the door because its members are presumed to know where it is, and Walker's is a kind of club, and some think a good one. So I paid off the taxi on the first sale day in April and went upstairs briskly to join the merry throng.

'Art'noon, Mr Straun.' Sid Walker, mine host for the afternoon, cautious blue eyes above the face of a Victorian prize fighter, rubbing big hands in welcome. 'Lookin' for anything special today, are we?'

'I'll have a nice used war bow, if you've got one, Mr Walker.' One does not call the brothers Walker by their given name, even if that's the way you think of them.

Sid grinned ferociously. 'You will 'ave your little joke, sir. A used war bow would be quite something, now, wouldn't it? Bloody 'undreds of new ones, thanks to the *Mary Rose*, but nobody's ever found a used one yet, far as I know. Funny, innit?' He led the way into the body of the kirk, so to speak. Walker's, according to legend, had been a Victorian billiard hall and now it was run much on the lines of a small-town auction room, with its wares set out round the walls and the punters' seats in the middle. Sid paused in front of a suit of armour. 'Nice, innit? Strictly kosher, too. Though I reckon one *couter* and the *poleyns* is Parrot.'

'Well,' I said, 'I don't see anyone getting upset about that.' The Parrots were the hereditary armourers at a castle in the Welsh Marches; Fred, the present incumbent, restoring the work of his ancestors and also, given the time, producing fresh suits of plate made with the same metal, wrought with the original tools, in the same forge. When Sid said that one of the elbow joints of this particular suit was the work of a twentieth-century Parrot instead of one who happened to have lived four centuries before, the difference was of time, not authenticity.

Sid said hopefully, 'There's a spanning rack for a crossbow somewhere. You might like to 'ave a look.'

I was a bit off crossbows but I didn't want to hurt his feelings, supposing that he had any. But then one never knew with the Walkers. It was common knowledge that they had started their careers behind a street barrow, but that hardly explained their encyclopædic grasp of the art market. It was rumoured that they'd picked it up in prison, sharing a cell with a forger from Amsterdam, but that seemed unlikely. In fact, more than unlikely, because I'd once looked the pair of them up in the form book and neither of them had ever been inside unless it was in another country and under another name. Sometimes I wondered if perhaps they had both gone to Eton and their robust exterior was just carefully cultivated window-dressing, but I suspected it would do considerable harm to our relationship if I tried too hard to find out.

'Now if you've gotta minute—' Sid was saying. He steered me towards his office, a holy place guarded by an ancient crone crouched over an even more ancient typewriter. I'm not quite sure what I was expecting. Greed being an essential part of the human condition, I suppose I thought I was going to be offered something particularly desirable that would not be available to anyone else. Like a bow certified to be the one that was used to inflict gay King Richard's mortal wound, or an arrow that had been part of the arrow storm at Agincourt. Or whatever. It's no wonder mediæval fly boys made such a handsome living flogging pieces of the True Cross.

Sid was saying, 'We are wonderin', Mr Straun, if you could give Geoff an' I a bit of an 'and over something. You being a policeman—'

After the rather satisfying success of a couple of historical novels, I was beginning to regard myself as a writer of renown rather than a policeman, but apparently the word hadn't got around. Once a copper always a copper, and a good one, like a good villain, goes quietly when he knows his time has come. Short of marching out of the office and never entering the gallery again, there really wasn't much I could do about it, but I mentally cursed Sid and all his kind. Aloud, I asked cautiously, 'What's the trouble?'

'The name's Smith.'

'Really Smith?'

Sid shrugged his shoulders. 'I wouldn't be surprised. If you're on the fiddle and you didn't want to use your own name you'd think up something a bit better than Smith, stands to reason.'

'I'll take your word for it,' I said. 'What's your trouble with Mr Smith, anyway?'

''E nicks stuff.'

'What, here in the saleroom?' I was genuinely surprised. Apart from the fact that saleroom thefts are comparatively rare, one got the feeling that it would be a brave man who tried to rob the Walker brothers, who looked as though they had a trick or two of their own. After all, who wants to get his arm broken in a dark alley when he could be at home looking at the box?

Sid said aggrievedly, 'Yes, here in the bloody saleroom! And him a dealer, too.' He corrected himself. 'Of sorts.'

I found it genuinely hard to picture a dealer stealing the silver, so to speak, and with so many of the public about, there didn't seem any desperate need for them to prey on each other. I asked, 'Why do you say "of sorts"?'

'Well, it's on 'is card.' Sid shrugged his shoulders. 'Got a small place in Islington, selling a load of this an' that. Some's all right, some ain't. But he buys regular from us.'

'You mean,' I said, 'he actually pays for some of it?'

'Pays for most of it,' Sid agreed, 'that's the trouble. If 'e didn't, I'd have told 'im to piss off long ago. 'E just takes the odd thing and puts it in 'is pocket as though 'e's entitled to it. Small stuff. It ain't the money, Mr Straun, it's the principle.'

I said, 'Then why not tell him not to do it?'

'Well, for one thing, 'e wouldn't come any more and 'e's not a bad customer.' Sid looked ill at ease and it occurred to me that he was genuinely embarrassed.

'Look,' I said, 'you'd do far better getting someone local in. All you've got to do is to have a word with the desk at Savile Row—'

'Then it would be official, wouldn't it, Mr Straun?' Sid looked at me hopefully. 'Now, if you could just have a word —let 'im know someone's on to 'im, so to speak—'

I said, 'If he's a kleptomaniac, *nothing's* going to stop him except proper treatment.' But I knew that was nonsense because one doesn't have kleptomaniac art dealers, at least not for very long. But it was just on the cards that Mr Smith might be a little sticky-fingered. Could happen to anybody. 'All right,' I said, 'point him out to me and I'll see what I can do.'

'I appreciate that, Mr Straun.'

'I don't guarantee results,' I told him. 'If he doesn't take the hint, there's not much more I can do about it. I'm an out of town copper and the local firm won't be amused if I move in on their home ground.'

Sid looked slightly hurt. 'Not even if you saw a murder?'

'I wouldn't *see* a murder on someone else's patch,' I assured him. 'So let's have a look at your Mr Smith.'

We went out into the saleroom and I studied the crowd. They come all sorts at Walker's, probably the largest group being retired services. Mr Smith was small and plumpish, spectacles and a dark suit.

I asked, 'What does he go for?'

'Bit of this, bit of that,' Sid told me gloomily. ''E's been 'aving a look round the marine stuff today.'

We went over and had a look at what turned out to be a smallish collection of artefacts, mainly Tudor. There was a nice collection of Spanish coins, properly boxed and obviously bought up as part of a collection. I poked over ancient rigging blocks and tools, seafarers' plates and basins, wine jars and cannon balls. I picked up a billiard-ball-sized missile with the barnacles still on it and weighed it in my hand.

'Carronade ball,' Sid said. 'The others is cast iron, that's lead.' He showed me a kite-shaped knife mark where someone must have tried to scrape away the tiny shells.

I asked him where it had come from, toying with the idea of buying it for Laurie as a paperweight. Sid shrugged his shoulders. 'I don't ask no questions, Mr Straun. There's plenty of wrecks around the coast, as you know. They're Crown property, of course, but people are always willing to risk a dive without a licence.'

Mr Smith in his blue suit went past, his eyes on the numbered Lots. He looked about forty, pale-faced and anonymous to the point where he could have been a bit film player made up as a downtrodden railway clerk. Sid gave me a discreet nudge. Well, I could see what he meant about the name. Personally I'd have laid good money on it being Smith. Come to that, it was pretty hard to imagine him being called anything else.

'All right,' I promised. 'I'll keep my eye on him.'

Come three o'clock we sat down and the sale started. The Walkers didn't bother with a rostrum; whichever brother happened to be officiating simply walked round the room with a clerk in attendance, offering the Lots as he reached them. Today the auctioneer was Geoff, a slightly smaller version of Sid and clearly off the same barrow.

'All right, gents, let's get on with it.' He selected a nasty-looking knife and showed that he meant what he said. 'Lot One. Nice rondel dagger, fifteenth-century Itie, etched blade an' very nice if you like that sort of thing. Looks like it might be by Fideli, but that's up to you. Leather sheath with brog goes with it an' if someone will start me at a grand I'll say thank you very much.'

Someone started him at five hundred but the thing had made thirteen hundred and fifty within about three minutes and we were on to the crossbow rack. I'd rather lost my enthusiasm for crossbows but I bought a hauberk hook that

Geoff said was Norman and was probably right. I sat back and listened to wealthy people investing small fortunes in plate armour and consoled myself with the thought that a policeman, even a policeman who happened to be a flukishly successful writer of historical novels, couldn't get himself too involved in that sort of thing.

Geoff Walker had got rid of his armour and was about to embark on golfiana.

'Nah then, a featherie or two—'   .

Policing is a job, writing a curiously lucrative hobby, but golf—golf is a way of life. Like anyone else who plays, I can spend a happy hour looking at museum pieces and wondering what it must have been like to play with them. I genuinely envied the player who got drunk as a skunk after winning the Open and went out in the middle of the night to play a few holes with a hickory-shafted club and a feather-filled ball he'd lifted out of a glass case in the host club's museum. But wondering was about as close as I was likely to get to it, old golf gear having rocketed in price like vintage cars once the investment boys moved in.

'Featherie by Tom Morris, certified 1850,' Geoff was saying. 'A'right, gents. Start me at a couple of 'undred.'

From somewhere right at the back of the hall a rich American voice said, 'One seventy-five.'

I looked round. He must have come in late because he certainly hadn't been there before the sale started, but there he was, sitting at the end of an empty row of seats at the back of the room, Chas. A. MacLiven as large as life.

On and off, I'd known Chas for a long time. He was an American resident, expatriate Scot who had played a lot of amateur golf in the early 'seventies until he had finally taken the plunge and turned professional. I'd played against him a lot in the days before he joined the PGA, and although he'd never been all that successful on the circuit he'd always

been the kind of extrovert, well-liked character who earned
his appearance money. He'd given the impression of never
having been short of a penny or two, so when he'd vanished
from the competition scene I'd assumed that he'd simply
grown tired of it. And if he was now prepared to open the
bidding at a hundred and seventy-five pounds for a single
unusable golf ball, it looked very much as though I'd been
right.

I listened while he bought a couple of balls, a driving
mashie, an ancient brassie, two sand niblicks and a cleek
by Old Tom Morris, the sum total of which must have come
to the thick end of four thousand pounds. I wondered
vaguely where the money was coming from as I hadn't even
seen his name in a tournament line-up for at least a couple
of years, let alone ending in the big prizes.

Walk back along the lines of seats at Walker's and you
have a chance to study what one imagines are known as the
punters to Sid and Geoff. It was a thing I couldn't remember
doing before and it struck me forcibly that we were a mixed
lot. At the big rooms you get mainly dealers and with an
art dealer you can tell the good, the bad and the ugly from
the other side of a wide street, whereas at Walker's most of
us are doing our own buying. Women, by and large, don't
seem to get involved, although on this occasion there were
a few lost-looking souls, wondering what it was all about.

There were some seats empty, so I dropped down beside
Chas.

'Angus, for Chrissake! Must be years.' Chas hadn't
altered much. Age-wise, he was probably getting on for fifty,
a big, fair-haired raw-boned character who looked as though
he might have been a cowboy from Wyoming, whereas in
fact he was a pure-blooded Scot who'd spent by far the
greater part of his life in the States. Like most converts, he
tended to play the American accent somewhat larger than
life, but what harm?

I said, 'It's not like a canny Scot to pay two hundred quid for a ball he can't use. You starting a museum or something?' There were several rows of empty seats in front of us, so it wasn't difficult to talk.

Chas grinned. 'Hell, you're a canny Scot yourself, come to that, laddie. And yes, I guess you could say I'm starting a museum. Or finishing it. It's a fair way along.'

'In Florida?' So far as I could remember, his home had been somewhere near Daytona, which seemed an odd place for a museum.

'Are you crazy?' Chas looked quite shocked. 'I don't live in the States any more. Promised myself years ago that as soon as I'd finished with the tour circuit I'd come back and look after Sarne.'

I did my best to remember what I'd heard about Chas's background and managed to recall that Sarne was one of those remote islands somewhere west of Skye. Chas had joked about it in the old days, eternally grateful that on the death of his father at the end of the war he'd been packed off to live with relatives in America. Golf had got him at an early age and he'd never had any incentive to leave his adopted home.

I asked, 'Wasn't there a castle, or something?'

Chas nodded. 'There was and is. Been shut for years, but not any more.

'And you're what—chief of the clan?'

'Aye. The MacLiven.' Just for that moment he sounded much as his father might have done. Perhaps it wasn't so wildly improbable after all, to have an American golf pro as a captain of the glens.

'Then what's this about a museum?'

'I'm turning the castle into a hotel—one hell of a lot of atmosphere it's going to have, too. A museum room looks good in a place like that.'

I couldn't see Sarne proving exactly handy for the

weekend traveller. 'For God's sake, Chas,' I protested, 'how are people going to get there?'

'You've heard of helicopters?' He let that one sink in before he added, 'There's a nine-hole golf course waiting to go. You want to come up and have a round or three? That reminds me, I'm fixing a Pro-Am day—how about you play in it?'

'Great!' I said. 'Love to.' It did indeed sound as though it might be fun but I wasn't giving him my whole attention because Geoff Walker had got to the maritime stuff and was holding up a wedge-shaped quoin that at some time had been used to elevate a gun barrel.

I said, 'Hang on a moment, Chas, I want to hear this sale.' The quoin had survived remarkably well, considering the fact that it had been under water for nearly four centuries, and I listened to the bidding with interest. There isn't a great deal one can do with a quoin on its own, and without a cannon to go with it there's not much employment prospect beyond a doorstop. Nevertheless, it went for a hundred and seventy-five pounds to Mr Smith, who made a note of it in a little book. He'd moved close enough for me to read what he was writing if he'd held it up the right way, which of course he didn't.

'Catch the night express Friday night,' Chas was saying. 'I'll meet you.' Apparently he wasn't into quoins either.

I said, 'Fine!' Which coming from someone who avoided trains like the plague showed that my mind was on other things. But Smith interested me. I had no means of knowing whether he was buying for a client or simply for stock, but as the lots came and went I had to admit that he knew what he was after. Some of the items didn't interest him at all, but what he wanted, he got. On the few occasions he encountered fairly determined competition he just outbid it, and I got the impression that however lunatically high the price might go, he'd bid on to the bitter end. I forget what the case of Spanish coins fetched but I know it was a lot more than they were worth. I wondered what Laurie's carronade ball paperweight was going to make and waited for the bidding with some curiosity. Either the Lot had been withdrawn or Geoff overlooked it, because it never came up. Strictly speaking, I should have been shadowing Mr Smith and not chatting to the MacLiven.

'Look,' I said to Chas, 'do you want to wait till the end?'

He shook his head. 'No. Got what I want.'

'Give me ten minutes, then, and we'll go and have a drink somewhere,' I said. 'Just got a little business to attend to.'

'Sure.' Chas nodded expansively. 'Take your time.'

Geoff Walker was on to books now, so I walked over and had a look at the maritime Lots that were already being packed up by the handling staff. The carronade ball wasn't there; neither, so far as I could see, was Mr Smith.

I went into the office to pay for my hauberk. Sid and the old dragon with the typewriter gave me a jointly unfavourable look.

'Well,' Sid greeted me, 'did you see him do it?'

I said, 'Do what?' automatically, but really I knew without being told.

'The carronade ball. It's gone, hasn't it?'

'Yes,' I said, 'it's gone.' It was my own fault, I should never have got involved.

'In that case,' Sid said bitterly, ''e must 'ave got the thing in 'is bleeding pocket.'

We looked at each other. I said weakly, 'You couldn't *get* a thing like that in your pocket.'

'You couldn't put a pheasant in your pocket neither, but a poacher does,' Sid told me.

I sighed. 'Sorry. I didn't realize he was that good.'

'He's good all right,' Sid said. 'Makes you wonder why he goes to all that trouble, just for something worth a few quid.' He sighed. 'Just as well, as it's the last we'll see of it.'

I agreed with him, which, as things turned out, meant we were both wrong. Nevertheless, there was something too novel about an antique dealer with kleptomania for me to let it go. Curiosity is an odd impulse. The Walkers had already assured me that Smith was a perfectly sound and respectable dealer, his little weakness excepted, so why did I have an urge to see his premises? I didn't for a moment doubt that they existed. Almost certainly they'd look exactly like a hundred other flourishing Islington enterprises, apart from the fact that the name 'Smith' would be above the door. All the same, there was something to be said for the desert general who made his plans with a photograph of his opposite number pinned up in front of him. Know your enemy. Was Mr Smith my enemy? Well he certainly wasn't my good friend.

Inevitably I went to Islington. Sid Walker had provided the address and sure enough, there it was. *A. Smith: Antiques*, a small, double-fronted shop done out in faded green paint, sandwiched in between *L. Spurgeon: Rare Books* and *Alice's Video*. I looked in the left-hand window and admired a couple of rather nice seventeenth-century games tables, some nondescript china and a battered ship's binnacle that I suspected came from a computer-controlled repro factory in Norfolk. But in fairness there were some pieces of good plate armour and several weapons that looked good, at least from a distance. Not a cannon ball in sight and the entrance bore a small card that said CLOSED.

Oh well. I walked back across the street, paused and glanced over my shoulder. A curtain in the window above the shop twitched. But soft, we are observed. All right, you little bastard, have a good look at me while you're at it. I turned round and faced the shop with some fuzzy idea that if he knew he was under observation he might mend his ways. It would have served me right if Mr Smith had leaned out of the window and waved, but of course he didn't and I suppose I'd have been surprised if he had.

CHAPTER 2

Over breakfast next morning I reviewed the day with a light heart, an indulgence for policemen but all right if they are on leave. Particularly all right in my case because the sun was shining and Laurie was sitting across the kitchen table from me and feeding bread into the toaster in a wifely way. Why does one say 'wifely', I wonder. Angela, that wife no longer, had been wifely with dire results. Laurie was a phenomenon I didn't want to probe too deeply as yet in case it got up and walked away.

'All right,' the phenomenon said, 'so the Ireland trip is off and we're going to some Scottish island instead.'

Conscience pricked. These last few weeks in London I'd been kept pretty busy co-ordinating an anti-terrorist course, presumably my legacy from the Kariba assassination attempt.* I'd quite enjoyed it, though I could have done without my picture in the papers, however much it cheered public relations. Still, I'd earned this leave and Laurie had been looking forward to it. Now I'd related my failure as a store detective for the Walker brothers in some detail and she'd enjoyed it, but clearly the Scottish offer was not going down so well. A little late, I said, 'I'm sorry about the change. You don't mind, do you?'

'Oh, I don't *mind* exactly.' Laurie pushed fair hair out of her eyes. Without her glasses she looked fetchingly defence-less and a good deal lower-powered than she was. 'Tell me

* *Dead Ball.*

about this Chas character. Come to that, why do you call him Chas?'

I said, 'It's the way he signs himself, short for Charles. I suppose it seemed funny because it's all very American and he's just a pure Scot at heart.'

'But American enough to want to turn this place he's inherited into a sort of Disneyland.'

'Or Scot enough to want to make it pay its way,' I told her. 'And you've probably got the wrong idea about Scottish castles—they don't come very big. Just right for a small hotel, and with his name Chas would be mad not to have a nine-hole golf course. People will pay a tidy bit just to say they've had a lesson or two from him, for a start.'

'And what about me?'

A woman-like thing to say, as I should have known, having known them, on and off, for some time. Long enough at any rate to have learned not to say what I did say, which was, 'Well, what about you?'

'Chas knows you're divorced? I mean, this island could hardly be better placed for a discreet weekend, could it? What did you say? *"All right if I bring—?"*'

'Now look,' I said, 'when Chas invited me I just said I'd been going to Ireland with a friend. And *he* said, "Well, you'd both better come here instead. There are a couple of rooms in the tower going begging."'

'He'll expect Angela.'

I said, 'Chas was someone I knew on the golf circuit, and I haven't even met him for years. He certainly never met Angela and I doubt if he even knew if I was married, let alone divorced. Men aren't like women—business acquaintances can know each other for bloody years without ever asking each other who they sleep with.'

'Oh, bully for you.' Laurie buttered toast with more care than the job really needed. Women's moods are unaccountable sometimes. 'How do we get there?'

'Up the M6 to Penrith. Then Glencoe, Fort William and the ferry to Skye. Chas picks us up at a place called Ardrossan in the chopper.'

'I thought you wanted to get on with the book.' Which was Laurie Wilson, my literary agent and adviser speaking. Unfair to switch roles, as well she must have known.

I said, 'I was giving it a couple of weeks' rest while we went to Ireland, so what's the difference?' I added, perhaps unwisely. 'Besides, Chas's castle has an oubliette I'd like to see.'

'You mean there isn't one nearer than the Western Isles?'

'Not in as good nick as this one. Supposed to be unique.'

Laurie looked bored. 'You make it sound like a second-hand car.'

'*Much* harder to find!'

A local pigeon landed on the window ledge and rattled its beak on the glass. Laurie pushed up the sash and served it muesli with added raisins. 'A sort of dungeon.' She was talking to the bird, not me.

Write historical novels and it's hard not to acquire at least a certain expertise with your chosen period. 'An oubliette was more like a dry well than a dungeon,' I explained. 'The prisoner got chucked in through a trapdoor. Once in, you weren't expected to come out. That's how they got their name—oublier—French for "forget".'

'I wonder what mediæval wit thought that up.' I wondered too, sitting there in the yellow twentieth-century sunshine, catching some ghost of a chill from an old evil. Then after a while she asked, 'So when do we go?'

'We could go today if the car's ready,' I told her. 'I'd better get round to the garage and see.'

Laurie said hopefully, 'We could go by train.' She had an inexplicable liking for trains that I did not share.

'We'll see.' Of course I had no intention of seeing. I put

a jacket on and went out into the early spring sunshine. Laurie's flat was in Kinnerton Street, just off Hyde Park Corner, and as usual the sound of London traffic fighting three ways at once made me grateful for the fact that I was a Wessex bumpkin. The mews where the car was being serviced was off Bayswater Road, so I walked across the park to kill time, not sure of London garage opening hours. I need not have worried, because when I arrived there were no less than three overalled backsides bent over my Maserati Mistrale. I felt a familiar wave of apprehension. With a labour rate of twenty pounds an hour, one backside is bad enough, three twenties make sixty, which means a day's work will come to the thick end of five hundred quid. Still, as Laurie was apt to say, this was what I wrote books for.

'Ah, Mr Straun. Good morning, sir.'

There is a lot to be said for the specialist, one make garage. It may charge the earth but by and large it instils a certain confidence. I had never dealt with Peregrine Motors before, but they knew my name and their overalls were clean. The garage itself consisted of a series of Georgian coach-houses, all knocked into one but still with the original granite setts for floor. At this establishment they dealt only with Maseratis, and beyond my own disembowelled Mistrale I could see a Ghibli, two Mexicos and the unclothed network of fine gauge tubing that was some-body's competition Birdcage. The cars were spotless, the tools shone. There was an air of competence and pride of craft that was once common enough, depressingly rare now.

The foreman was a brisk sort of chap who knew exactly what was wrong and said so. 'The thrust race has gone on the clutch, as I thought. But there's oil getting in too, from the main bearing.'

I hadn't noticed the characteristic thump of that particular ill and said so, suitably humbly.

'Oh, you can't *hear* it, sir. But you can feel it.' He could, at least.

I said resignedly, 'So that means getting the engine out.' The Lord alone knew what that would cost in labour.

He said sympathetically, 'Well, we can drop the box and get at the clutch that way. But as the crankshaft will have to come out, it'll probably be quicker in the long run to lift the block.'

'Well,' I said, 'you'd better do what's best. Have you got the bearings?'

'They're on order.' He sounded sufficiently confident for me to be quite sure they were. Without waiting for me to ask the obvious, he went on, 'With any luck they should be here this week. After that, a couple of days' work.'

'Thanks,' I said, 'I'll keep in touch.' It would have been fun to have taken the Mistrale up north—it was a new toy to me and I still jumped at any excuse to drive it. Oh well. Laurie, at least, would be pleased.

I could have gone back to tell her but I wanted to go to the London Library, so I went there instead. I could have telephoned, but there seemed very little point, it being the sort of thing one could talk about later, and I wasn't happy about the car.

Be that as it may, by the time I finally got back to Kinnerton Street it was in time to see Marcus Winter's personally number-plated Jaguar exiting left. Winter was a publisher of some renown, a smooth and beautifully controlled accountant who had made a name for himself reorganizing a pet food empire and was now doing the same thing in the book trade with total success. He was still in his thirties and looked as though he kept himself very fit, a combination of talents that had irritated me unreasonably on the few occasions we'd met.

'Look, darling, it seems Louis Akerman is going to be in Ireland next week after all, and Marcus is very keen to get one or two things sorted out and the wretched man won't answer letters.' I saw that Laurie had taken on her executive look. 'You remember I did say I might have to see him while we were over there.'

'Yes,' I said, 'I remember.' I did vaguely. Akerman was some kind of diplomat who seemed to have written a highly undiplomatic book. Laurie had said something about trying to see him while we were over there but I'd hoped it was the sort of hiccup that would go away.

'So I'll just have to go. I'm sorry about Scotland.'

'It can't be helped,' I said. 'I'll explain to Chas.'

She looked at me. 'You mean you're still going?'

'Well, I've said I'd play the Pro-Am and you'll be busy anyway.'

Looking back on it later, of course, I realized I'd had a clear choice of Chas's company or Laurie's and I hadn't chosen hers.

She said, 'Sometimes, Angus, you can be a bastard.'

'I'll buy you a good dinner.'

She ignored that. 'I'm surprised you're not off tonight.'

'Not for a couple of days,' I told her. 'I've got to go back to the nick for a few things first.'

Laurie bit her lip. 'I thought you were supposed to be on leave.'

'Something's cropped up on an inquiry I was on.' It was true. I'd checked in from the Library but she wasn't to know that.

I knew I was behaving badly and that it would get worse rather than better over dinner. If I'd stopped and reasoned I might have decided that after the messiness of the divorce I was wary of getting into too deep water with Laurie. Still, it wasn't the best of ways of declaring my independence, just one more of the follies some of us stumble into with fair regularity from the cradle to the grave.

*

'Coupe 3c,' the man said, taking my ticket. 'Right here, sir!'
He'd come from Jamaica way, or his father had, and he was
a happy steward, which is a thing one doesn't find all that
often. He took me along to my tiny private compartment,
bright blue upholstery, shiny woodwork, newer than I'd
expected. The miniature bathroom was clean, too. I gave
the happy steward something and he thanked me with lots
of white teeth and told me where the bar was. Breakfast
would be served in the restaurant car, but there were only
sandwiches available until then, not unreasonable since it
was ten o'clock at night.

I had a drink and went to bed and in the morning there
he was again, bright and smiling, bearing morning tea
in mock silver thingummies and telling me it was a nice
day.

I could see it was a nice day. Out there through the
window the sky was a pale chill blue but you could see for
ever over hundred-acre fields, while in the distance the hills
rose fuzzy against the skyline. The train was rocking steadily
with the kind of high-speed rhythm that seems peculiar to
British railway tracking, backed with a kind of feline diesel
growl.

'Where are we?' I hauled myself up in the narrow bed
and poured tea while he held the tray, one's obedient
servant, cheerfully willing to please.

'An hour to Crianlarich.' He made it sound like some
place in the Caribbean. 'We're running on time, and a fine
day.' He stood with his back to me, swaying gently as he
stared out of the window to make sure it was all right for
me. 'You take breakfast, sir?'

'Yes,' I said, 'I'll take breakfast.'

I took it, but I can't say that I enjoyed it, the much-
publicized private pot of marmalade notwithstanding. I was
not at ease on the subject of Laurie. A literary agent may
conceivably put up with a bloody-minded author in the way

of business, but not a bloody-minded lover as well. Not for
ten per cent. I thought of the next couple of days. Pro-Am
competitions are not everybody's cup of tea, and some
professionals get little fun out of being paired with some
glitzy show business personality with a handicap of twelve.
Well, too late to worry about that now, the deed was done.
I drank coffee and looked out of the window. We were
getting into the higher country now and the railway ran a
little above the road. On the steep bank leading down to it,
the odd sheep stared up at us incuriously, a rabbit here and
there. I wondered what Laurie was doing and if she was as
angry as she'd been the day I let myself in for this. Odd,
but I didn't know her well enough to know how long she
stayed on the boil. The sick feeling of having made a fool of
myself was no better at thirty-eight than it had been at
twenty, which just proves that some people never learn.

'More coffee, sir?'

I shook my head and the chap went away. Maybe the
best thing would be to telephone from Fort William, though
I wasn't sure I wanted to grovel over the phone. I surveyed
my fellow travellers and was rewarded with the usual mixed
bag, typical mini-tycoons chewing over their Filofaxes, a
few middle-aged couples, a fortyish, freewheeling gent in
jeans and a headband, plus a party of nuns. I was wondering
what bricks they might individually have dropped when a
heavyish, blue-chinned character in a rather nasty suit
caught my eye from the table across the aisle.

'Did you hear the news this morning?'

I shook my head. 'No.' How was one to hear the news on
a train? I supposed he carried his own radio, a habit that
seemed OK for the young but a bit unnecessary for an adult.
Did anyone really need to be that close to the news? Well,
this one did, obviously.

'The government's given in over the electricity strike.
That means all the rest will be trying their luck.'

As a race the British have an instinct for the proprieties and it is not done to talk politics with strangers, quite apart from the fact that these days you could end up with a good thumping. As a behaviour pattern it is so engraved that I actually found myself wondering if he could be a foreigner, but he spoke London English. Oh well. I said, 'That seems to be the general pattern,' doing my best to sound unenthusiastic without being totally offensive. I didn't want to be rude; equally I wanted him to go away.

'I always carry a radio with me, so that I don't miss the news.' He had dark, rather doggy eyes that were regarding me with what could have been amusement. Probably he guessed he was answering my unspoken question. He went on, 'My wife says I'm dead nosey—that I'm terrified of missing something.'

I said, 'She sounds a sensible woman.'

'She is. But then she *never* listens to the news. They could declare World War III and she'd never know.'

I told him it was probably just as well.

'True.' He pushed his coffee cup away. 'I must say, they do you a good breakfast still, even if it does cost an arm and a leg. Like the drinks in the buffet—'

The steward came with my bill. Had he been hiding somewhere and decided to come to my rescue? I imagined it was hardly likely but was glad to see him just the same.

'Hang on,' I said, 'I'll pay now.'

He hung on and I paid. As the man said, it cost an arm and a leg, but at least I'd enjoyed it.

'I didn't see you in the bar last night.'

All this would have been understandable if I'd been a woman, but I wasn't and there was nothing about either of us that wasn't pretty obviously heterosexual. I felt an inclination to be rude and shut him up but I put it down firmly and told myself that the poor sod couldn't help being lonely or friendly or whatever. I agreed that I hadn't been in the bar and got up to go. He dropped money on to the bill the steward had left him and got up too.

'At least we'll be in Fort William on time.'

I mumbled something. Presumably the steward had told him about the train or maybe he'd heard it on his private radio, but in any case I was so brainwashed by this time that I took it for granted he was right. I thanked God piously for the fact that I was travelling in my own sleeper and not an open compartment, otherwise there would have been no shaking him off. The thought cheered me so much that I decided that I could afford to be civil to the man for the few minutes of his company that remained, so we chatted in quite matey fashion as half a dozen of us rocked our way between the tables and out into the corridor.

'You know,' he said, 'I was born just about here. Never think it, would you?'

A Catch 22 question if ever there was one. In fact, the answer was 'No' because he neither sounded nor looked like a Scot. True, he must have been born somewhere and I had absolutely no better suggestion to make, largely because I simply didn't care. But that his mother delivered him here—

I said, 'No, you didn't strike me as being from these parts.'

'Just shows how wrong you can be, old man.' We'd passed the doors marked 'Toilet' and the concertina-like join that linked the restaurant car to the one behind it. At the door of the new coach he paused and bent to look out of the window. 'Born in Raffety, out there. Can't pretend you can see the house but you can see the church. Have a look.'

Well, there's one born every minute. I bent down to have a look at the view that included an embankment down to a field and in the distance some sort of village with the usual spire.

I said, 'Very nice.'

He didn't answer and I went on looking because it seemed polite. I was still looking when a heavy shoulder caught me in the back and slammed me against the window with such force that for a moment I was actually unconscious. Then a hand gripped the back of my collar and crashed my head back against the glass. I remember thinking how lucky the door was there to stop me falling out. But I was wrong because without warning it opened and swung free.

I fell endlessly through the screaming slipstream of the speeding train.

CHAPTER 3

There are worse things to fall down than a railway embankment, although I wasn't aware of that at the time. As I plummeted through the air I took in the grass-covered bank below me and somehow had time to feel relief that whatever happened I should at least not end up underneath the wheels of the train. I think I even felt a certain anger with myself for allowing such a thing to happen. No time for fear. Luckily I'd rolled out of a few moving vehicles, fallen down some stairs and, in any case, instinct is a handy thing, even though it was formed in the days before I acquired a dodgy arm. I drew my legs up, hugged my knees and buried my head in my chest.

A human ball, I hit the ground.

I have no idea how fast the train had been moving when I left it, but thirty miles an hour is about as fast as anyone can roll out of a car and hope to get away with it, and even that pre-supposes a landing on a tarmac road. The train was certainly going faster than that, but I landed downhill, on rough, tufted grass. Human balls don't bounce, but they roll like mad. I rolled like mad. It was a nightmare sensation, half horror at the thought of what was happening to me, half sheer relief that at least I was still alive. I hugged my knees desperately and tried not to think about what it would be like if I hit a tree. What it would be like if I hit *anything*.

I slowed. Only momentarily, but it seemed the moment to chance my luck. I unclasped my hands, straightened my legs, and rolled half a dozen times, full length, like a log, and a stone smacked me painfully on the jaw. I heard myself yelp and grabbed at thick grass as it sped past me, gripped and held on. My arm straightened and a joint cracked. Abruptly, all movement ceased.

I lay there, with my face in a patch of clover. In the background I could pick out the receding throb of the train, but it was a sound outside me, detached, the last knockings of another world. What was real was the scent of clover and a steady thudding that I finally recognized as the beating of my heart. I still didn't move and the sound of the train ebbed and died and in its place a blackbird began his song and some unidentified insect buzzed past my ear.

It seemed time to start straightening my legs in turn. It was a job I did cautiously, because I was dead scared about what I might find out but it seemed they were all right. I tried sitting up, and rather to my surprise I could do that too, although my left shoulder hurt like the devil. I prodded it with my right hand and was comforted by the fact that it smarted hotly, the schooldays-remembered sensation of an honest bruise and graze. And not only my shoulder. Christ! Isolated chunks of pain here and there on my back, which presumably came from rolling over stones, but no more than bruising, with any luck.

I stood up and an inquisitive sheep moved away unhurriedly. Standing was painful again but I didn't object, because pain meant I was still alive. I went carefully down the bank, with no ambition to fall over and start rolling

again. I brooded on the identity of the chatty sod who had
so confidently pushed me out into thin air. True, the police
weren't all that popular these days but usually they at least
stopped the train before they threw us out. I recognized the
euphoria of not being dead and knew that if there'd been
anyone around to talk to I'd have been chatting like mad.
Hold it, I thought.

All right, so an unknown man had tried to kill me. Now
try and work out why.

The question stayed with me but without producing
anything in the way of an answer. A policeman tied to the
administrative desk because years ago a shotgun-toting
villain had just about put paid to my right arm didn't even
have enemies to watch out for. By and large, criminals
harbour little resentment against chaps who spend their
working days fiddling with manning levels. Which still left
the fact that even today people tend not to knock each other
off just on impulse.

There was a road at the bottom of the bank, by no means
major but better than nothing at all, so I walked along it in
the direction the train had been going. Chatty had made
much of the fact that I hadn't been in the bar the evening
we'd started from King's Cross, which suggested he had
been on the look-out for me even then. Which would make
sense if I believed he had come aboard the train for the sole
purpose of killing me. As I'd stayed in my own compartment
he'd been forced to wait till the morning, and an hour from
Fort William had certainly been leaving things close. No
wonder Chatty had been so insistent. I walked on, glad to
feel the stiffness easing with each step. A car came up behind
me and stopped.

'Would you be wanting a lift or is it the exercise you're
after?' An elderly, nice Scots gentleman in a long-chassis
Land-Rover. I'd been prepared to flourish warrant cards
and the majesty of the law in exchange for transport but an

Aquascutum jacket and Moss Bros. whipcords survive falls from trains rather well and ensure an aura of respectability.

I said, 'Thank you. I'd be glad of a lift.'

'I'm going as far as Crianlarich.' If he wondered how I'd got as far as I had, he didn't show it.

'That would be fine.' I climbed aboard and sank back in the seat, trying not to wince. Tentatively I said, 'It's a fine morning.'

'Aye.' My garrulity must have had the desired effect because that was almost the last word I had from my companion until he put me down in the shadow of Crianlarich's neat little station.

'Thank you, I'm very grateful,' I said as I slammed the door, and meant it.

The old blue eyes regarded me dispassionately. 'You're very welcome.' He seemed to consider something for a moment. 'There's blood on your face.'

I put my hand up instinctively, and there was a soreness round my right jaw. 'Thanks,' I said, 'I didn't know.'

He nodded, engaged gear noisily, and was gone. I wished him well and bought myself a platform ticket at the station so that I could make use of its facilities to clean myself up. I was a little startled at what I saw in the mirror. The blood on my face was nothing, no more than the result of a few scratches and my jacket and shirt looked respectable enough, even if not particularly well pressed. But I realized why the owner of the Land-Rover had stared at me. Hard to define, but my face was not that of a man who'd just finished reading the morning paper. I wondered when I should see my luggage again.

By and large, British Rail is good with luggage, steering lost items into an appropriate place. But I imagined the guard must have wondered what had happened, as I'd not only vanished personally but abandoned my belongings as well. Presumably nobody had witnessed my undignified exit from the train, but BR must have taken the mystery in its stride, read the appropriate labels and acted accordingly. In fact the luggage almost beat me to Sarne, with untouched locks to suggest that Chatty had been interested only in knocking me off personally and could not have cared less about what I was carrying.

More than anything else at that moment I wanted a bath, and that being more than Crianlarich Station had to offer I did a deal with the hospitable landlord of a local inn. In comfortable privacy I confirmed that there was a raw patch on my shoulder the size of a saucer and various difficult to look at parts of my anatomy that were coming up in shades of purple and black. Well, it could have been worse, and for the first time I felt glad that Laurie had not been with me. The inn's bath was brass-tipped and magnificently old-fashioned but spotlessly clean, so I filled it up with scalding hot water and soaked blissfully for ten minutes, less an immediate indulgence than an insurance against total seizing up later in the day. After that I had a cup of coffee and went in search of transport to Fort William and Mallaig, from where I'd catch the ferry for the Isle of Skye, where a second boat would see me across to Sarne. Chas's ancestral home might have potential for a discreet weekend away but certainly not for a quick one.

The journey to Mallaig is reputed to be one of the scenic wonders of the railway world, but it's a long haul from Euston. It was noon before we reached Fort William, well into the afternoon by the time I boarded the Skye ferry at Mallaig, early evening before a hire car from Portree deposited me in front of the West Highland Hotel at Ardrossan.

'Shall I be taking your bag in for you, sir?' He was an earnest, obliging lad, my driver, keen to do well in the business he'd just started.

I said no, and paid him and he went away, leaving me wondering why I'd been so sure. How did one get to Sarne at five o'clock in the evening? Chas was to have met my original train but when I hadn't been on that, it seemed unlikely he'd just hang around for the next. I ran my eye around the tiny port, with its toy quay and semi-circle of low granite buildings, the screaming seagulls wheeling in the sky, with the dark bulk of the Cuillins as a background. Apart from a chap mending a fishing net against the sea wall, the only people around seemed to be walkers, laden with packs and field-glasses.

I went into the West Highland and asked the grey-haired woman in the cubby-hole marked 'Reception' how one got to Sarne.

'There's a boat that belongs to the hotel.' She studied me in not unfriendly fashion from behind sensible glasses. 'Would you be a friend of the MacLiven?'

I said yes, I was.

'You'd be Mr Straun, then?' And when I nodded, 'He was here to meet you a while back. He was wondering what might have happened to you.' It wasn't my fault but she made me feel guilty.

'I'm afraid I got held up. So how do I go about getting out to Sarne? Is there a telephone?' Was it reasonable to suppose there'd be a 'phone link to the island? Under the sea? I realized that I'd never given much thought to the actual mechanics of telephone engineering before.

The woman said unexpectedly, 'Aye, there's a telephone. But it's no working just now. It's not all that reliable.'

'I'm not surprised,' I told her. 'So where do you suggest I get a boat?'

'You could ask the divers.' I suppose I looked blank because her face broke into a smile, and surprisingly warm at that. 'Och, I'm sorry, I keep forgetting you've only just arrived. But there are some diving men who are having a boat. They were in Portree this afternoon, and they'll take you with them out to Sarne as like as not.'

'What kind of divers?' So far as I knew, there were no rigs in the area.

'Och, they're diving all the time in those black rubber things. They say there's an old wreck or something but I wouldn't know. If you go over to the quay you'll see them sure enough with that great boat of theirs.'

Just then I'd have approached the Devil himself if he'd got a big boat, so I thanked her and picked up my bag and walked back towards the quay. I was glad I'd come. The Strauns were Highlanders too, and I suppose there was something in the light that made even an expatriate feel at home. Travel as far north as Fort William and you feel the sky change, so that even when it rains, which it does frequently, a wet day in those parts is never quite the same as it is anywhere else. At night you see the hills thrown up against the flickering of the Aurora Borealis and at dawn the world glows with the luminosity of a stage set. It's a thing you think you remember when you're away from it but when you see it again in reality it comes fresh each time, and it felt good, walking along the granite with the old smell of the place in my nostrils.

If the Sea Chief had been an aircraft I suppose it would have been a C47 Dakota, a straightforward, unbreakable product that will go on doing whatever you ask of it year after year with unfailing reliability until someone sinks it or burns it or somehow manages to blow it up. It was a boat that first got off the drawing-board towards the end of World War II, when it was intended to be a new breed of light MTB. Too late to see action, it went on sale with an almost unlimited list of options and in a remarkably short time it was being bought all over the world. Excise officers loved it; come to that, so did smugglers. Thirty feet long, ready and willing to accept almost any marine engine you'd care to name, it was seaworthy, accommodating and capable of being made very fast. More than a few business tycoons filled it up with bunks and bars and used the thing as a high-speed mini yacht, although this was out of character. Most were on the pattern of the one I was looking at now, with a forward wheelhouse and a lot of open space aft. *Molly M* of Wexford. I noted air tanks and scuba gear, which was reasonably par for the course, because even an old Sea Chief is still worth good money and anyone who owns one is more than likely to be into some kind of marine sport. All the same, *Molly M* hadn't the look of a rich man's toy. She was sound enough, but the paint was scuffed and the brasswork hadn't been polished for a long time. One of the windows of the wheelhouse was cracked and the rest were either salt-encrusted or just plain dirty. Not so much a boat that had fallen on hard times as one that worked hard for a living and didn't get much in the way of thanks.

I called, 'Anyone aboard?'

A young man came up from the engine hatch, wiping his hands on an oil-stained towel. He was probably about twenty-five, with fair curly hair and the slightly sulky good looks of the kind of schoolboy parents call 'difficult'. The only thing he wore above a pair of filthy jeans was a flower-patterned headband, and his bare arms and shoulders were heavy with muscle. He looked at me without speaking and I saw that his eyes were light blue and vaguely disturbing. Not mad eyes. Not shifty. Not really anything immediately definable. I do not like thee, Doctor Fell. But then, nobody was asking me to like him and, anyway, I was the one who was trying to cadge a ride.

I said, 'My name's Straun. I'm a friend of Mr MacLiven and the people at the hotel said you might be able to help me get to Sarne.'

The boy rubbed his jaw with the back of a tattooed hand. He had the long upper lip of the Irishman of political cartoons and there was the appropriate lilt in his voice as he said unexpectedly, 'Patrick.'

Patrick emerged from the saloon like someone who'd been in the wings.

'Are you wantin' me, Sean?'

There were two of them. Same face, same body, same jeans, same headband. Strange how disturbing identical twins can be. One wonders what it's like to have a mirror image. And do they really think alike?

Sean said, 'It's a Mr Straun. Could we be giving him a ride to the island?'

They looked at each other. Perhaps they were telecommunicating a discussion as to whether they liked the look of me or not. Eventually latecomer Patrick nodded. 'Why not?' To me he said, 'We were after leaving some gear there. If you'd like to come aboard, we'll go now.'

I slung my bag over the side and followed it down to the deck. I said, 'Thanks, it's good of you.'

'We was going anyway.'

I pushed my bag where it wouldn't be in the way and sat on it. I asked, 'How do people manage when you're not here?'

'You can ring for the hotel boat when the phone's working,' Sean told me. 'And MacLiven's got a chopper.'

'Has he now?' I had forgotten just how thoroughly Chas had apparently got the bit between his teeth. God knows how much one had to pay for a helicopter of one's very own but I imagined it would buy a whole stable of Maseratis. Why had I abandoned a promising golf career to be a policeman? Coppers couldn't buy helicopters out of their pay. Nor, come to that, could most golfers. I asked Sean who piloted the thing.

'MacLiven.'

Not Mr MacLiven or The MacLiven. MacLiven. I wondered if it was familiarity or dislike, but not for long, because there were lines to be cast off before the engines woke with an even growl and we headed out into the grey Atlantic.

A Sea Chief makes an impressive ferry, a big enough craft to give anyone aboard a feeling of security and comfort while at the same time exhibiting a surge of power of the kind one usually expects from a ski boat. There was no sensation of the bow coming up and the hull beginning to ride on the step, it was just a matter of vast, progressive acceleration as though one was being towed by a whale. White water slashed back on either side, forming a great V that seemed to stretch for ever and the wake from the twin screws boiled and churned for what looked like a mile behind us. I imagine most Sea Chiefs are steered from the comfort of the plush indoors, but Patrick—or was it Sean? —stood at the deck controls, and I didn't blame him. It was a nice toy to have under your hands on a fine day, with the Cuillins at your back and a couple of hundred blobs of island scattered about for no other apparent reason than that they looked good. The note of the engines had steadied to a resonant background growl and the only other sound was the banging of the odd rogue wave that battered for a moment against the bow before being thrown off in a burst of spray. I sat and admired the way the sunlight broke up the droplets of water into little rainbows and the dip and swoop of the big black-backed gulls that were doing an escort job.

Sean came by, identifiable by tattoos, and I said, 'They sound good.'

'Och, they're all right.'

'Chryslers?'

He braced himself against the movement of the deck. 'You're knowing boats?'

'Boats, no,' I said. 'A little about engines.'

We talked about engines, which he understood pretty well. I nodded towards the air tanks and the rest of the gear.

'What are you diving for?'

His mouth smiled. 'Come now, Mr Straun, surely you must be knowing that.'

I said, 'You'll have to forgive my shortcomings, but I'm new to these parts.'

'It's off the old quay at the end of the point.' He jerked his head to the north. 'An old Armada wreck.'

'I didn't know there was one up here.' And I hoped there wasn't, there being too many wrecks already being ruined by submarine cowboys jumping in with both feet when a delicate probe would be more than enough.

Sean said casually, 'Oh, there's one there right enough. The *Santa Marina*.'

'You've found her?' I had to shout to make myself heard.

Sean nodded before turning away to talk to Patrick. Either he had no intention of telling me anything more or he was just bored, so I settled down to admire the view of Sarne coming up out of the mist with the sun beginning to set behind it. The west coast of Scotland isn't short on offshore islands and I can't say that Chas's looked very different from all the rest. Seen from water level it looked like a giant inverted pudding basin, with the sea churning at the base of granite cliffs. Staring into the light, it was impossible to tell how much green there was on the place because it showed as no more than a black lump against the sky. It seemed a hell of a place for a hotel and I wondered if Chas was right and people were really going to pay good money to go there.

One of the Irish boys pointed to the island and shouted something.

'Yes,' I said, 'thank you.' Neither of us could hear the other, and I felt like whoever it was in Dickens who was always shouting at his dotty father. Quite apart from the fact that there was something uncomfortably decisive about leaving the mainland behind. *Suffer a sea change, into something rich and strange*—So what was I doing here, anyway? I was helping out a dear old pal. I was also playing fast and loose with my personal relationships and people were pushing me out of trains.

One of the twins came over and shouted in my ear. 'Ten minutes!'

I nodded. We were getting near in now and taking a course round the eastern end of the island. Seen close to, the cliffs were appalling and it seemed impossible that anyone could even land on the place. The Sea Chief grunted and lurched in the eddies, little hatfuls of brine splashed over the deck and the steady rise and thrust of the boat's progress changed abruptly to a nightmare corkscrewing motion. It had been a long time since I'd had anything to do with boats and I concentrated hard on something else. Fortunately it didn't last long, because we turned round the end of the island, the engines were throttled back and we were creeping forward at the speed of an ordinary fishing-boat. I looked over my shoulder and for the first time I set eyes on Chas's castle.

One imagines that the island had been made habitable by some ancient rock fault that had split an otherwise solid chunk of granite and allowed a great wedge to fall off into the sea, leaving a kind of step by way of which the first settlers must have made their way to the grassy plateau on which they had for centuries raised sheep. Nature had done the job more neatly than one might have expected, because a few cottages nestled handily on the step, its face forming a natural sea wall for the tiny quay. The backdrop to the hamlet was almost perpendicular stone, save for the western corner which must have suffered in the general collapse and had become sufficiently fractured for someone to have cut rough steps that wound upwards and out of sight. As a place at which to disembark it was a cross between an aircraft carrier and an oil rig.

The Sea Chief nosed the mooring and Patrick threw a
line ashore and someone on shore wove the line round a
bollard and I picked up my bag and threw it to land. Sean
was the nearest, so I paused before jumping ashore and
thanked him for the trip.

'A pleasure, Mr Straun. Isn't it good now, you've come
to see us?'

I met his cold blue stare and all at once I knew why it
was so familiar. Long ago, outside a bank, I'd stared into
eyes with just the same expression. Only on that occasion
their owner had been squinting along the barrel of a sawn-off
shotgun just a fraction of a second before he pulled the
trigger.

CHAPTER 4

A Land-Rover made its entrance OP with maximum sound
effects, skidded to a halt centre stage and deposited the lead
character.

'For Chrissake!' Chas demanded, 'where you *bin*?'

He was nothing like any Chas MacLiven I'd ever known,
a Chas in tweed jacket and a kilt. Not only a kilt but a
sporran, long hose with a *skean dhu* and brogues that looked
as though they weighed about five pounds apiece. To anyone
who had met him in his previous incarnation, he was
ridiculous, but then how does one judge these things? To a
newly arrived guest at the hotel he was probably quite
charismatic. Chas was by no means small, and the Highland
gear sat on him well enough. At least no crowd gathered to
laugh at the sight, so I didn't either.

'I had troubles,' I said.

'I believe it. Only just got the chopper back from the Kyle
or I'd have made it back for another go.' Out of sight

below the edge of the quay the Sea Chief's engines gurgled throatily and Chas's face twisted into uncharacteristic venom. 'You're not telling me you came with those Irish sons of bitches.'

'I asked them if they could give me a lift,' I said, 'and they did.'

'You're goddam lucky the bastards didn't cut your throat.' Chas picked up my clubs and bag and dumped them in the back of the Land-Rover. He got behind the wheel. 'Move it and I'll buy you a dram.'

'What's the trouble with the Heavenly Twins?' I had to shout because he was already grinding the starter.

Chas bared his teeth. 'Funny you calling them that. Kirstie does, too.'

I got in beside him just in time. 'Kirstie?'

'Kirstie Stewart,' Chas said, 'is the future Mistress Mac-Liven.'

It was a good line and he didn't try to improve on it. Instead we made a wild circuit of the quay and left the way he'd come, tyres scrabbling on the loose surface of the little track that started behind one of the cottages and wound upwards until we reached the high plateau of the island and there right ahead of me was Sarne Castle. Or as the very new signboard had it:

THE SARNE CASTLE
GOLF HOTEL

'Some place,' Chas was saying with satisfaction. He braked to a noisy stop in the gravelled courtyard and I got out and had a look at what some distant ancestor of his must have been a long time making. I knew it was a castle because that was what Chas called it, although apart from a few crenellations I can't say it had a lot in common with the kind of thing the Queen has at Windsor. But then, we Scots are a frugal race and we built our castles for function rather than for show. A laird who got around to raising any kind of fortress at all did so in order to be able to sleep reasonably safely at night, and maybe have himself a tower from which he could overlook the local countryside. He didn't hold court in it, and he didn't require it to accommodate several hundred men at arms. He didn't *have* that many and, in any case, in Scotland the siege as a form of warfare was virtually unknown. The classic Norman castle, with its donjon and enceinte, its curtain walls and flanking towers, was a small fortified town, but north of the border a castle could be anything from a basic keep to a fortified house.

The Castle Golf Hotel was a cross between the two, a bleak, grey, rainwashed building carved out of chunks of granite. The major part was a simple keep-like pile, with a massive door, arrow slits, and a general appearance of having been there for at least a thousand years. At some later date a lower building had been tacked on, with rather fancy oriel windows and a couple of mini-turrets for good measure. By normal castle standards it was tiny, but in its day it must have been well nigh impregnable, perched as it was on the edge of a hundred-foot-high cliff. As a modern hotel it looked about as welcoming as a prison and twice as cold, but who was I to say that?

'Haven't got around to doing anything to the outside yet,' Chas said, apparently having the ability to read my mind, 'but I fixed the interior real nice.'

We went in, and he was right. Chas had fixed his ancestral seat within an inch of its life. As in most keeps, the ground floor was built around a single room, once the great hall, which had been turned into the dining-room of a kind that would look well in a brochure. The fireplace, probably original, was geared to roast an ox, but the stone walls were covered with so many targes and claymores that a MacLiven of old could easily have equipped a sizeable raiding force from stock. They were all fakes and not particularly good ones, but I hardly imagined the customers either knew or cared. The floor was flagged, plentifully strewn with expensive-looking rugs, and the odd suit of quite genuine sixteenth-century armour stood around looking slightly embarrassed amid the Highland splendour, quite apart from being a century adrift into the bargain. But what the hell, it was warm and lush and even if the bar was upholstered in tartan, which it was, the customers obviously liked it that way. The place was comfortably full of well-heeled-looking people, all with accents a million miles away, which was probably just as well.

It was as we entered the bar that a small, grey-haired little man with large horn-rimmed glasses, who looked as though he'd stepped straight out of *Wind in the Willows*, was repacking one of those camera cases that have an abiding fascination for Customs officers.

Chas paused at his table. 'You had a good day?'

The little man smiled. He had a round, creased face and eyes that looked huge behind the thick lenses. 'Thank you, yes. Real good.' His voice vaguely American, first generation something or other, soft and self-effacing. A cuddly little chap.

'Max Meuse is our photography buff,' Chas informed me.

I looked into the open case at the couple of Nikon F4 bodies and an assortment of long lenses, including a 400mm that must have set him back the thick end of a thousand quid. I'd read somewhere that the average American enthusiast spends nearly three times that on his hobby every year, and I was beginning to see how he did it.

'What have you been taking?' I asked.

Mr Meuse smiled gently. 'Your beautiful country. The light, you know. The light on the hills is very remarkable.'

Chas said, 'You know we got a darkroom, special for guests? You want to use it, just say.'

'Sure,' Mr Meuse said. 'You're very kind.'

Chas patted his shoulder. 'Just want to see you got everything.'

It was a new Chas MacLiven. What he was saying was trite 'mine host' stuff but transparently he meant it. All those years a golfer with a hotelier trying to get out.

'Tell me about this Kirstie,' I said as we sat down. The barman, in plaid, had brought us large doses of malt in cut glass so heavy it needed two hands to lift it.

'You'll meet her at dinner.' Chas was not quite with me, but he must have had more things to do than sit passing the time of day. He made an effort. 'I hadn't expected you to be alone.'

'Something cropped up at work, and Laurie had to stay in town,' I said. 'She sends her apologies.'

'There's a room next to yours in case she finds she can make it.' Which was nice of him; strange how one can underrate one's friends. I was going to ask him about the golf but someone else wanted to talk to him about something so I said I'd see him at dinner and went up to my room to have a bath and change.

Whoever had done the refurbishing job for Chas had been consistent, because the bedrooms were like the rest of the place, only more so. Did the lords of the glen sleep in vast four-poster beds? I doubted it, just as I was absolutely sure they didn't pad around in ankle-deep Wilton or resort to bathrooms with onyx bidets, but it was lavishly comfortable none the less. The room next door had an elm tester and apple-green carpeting and I thought what fun it would have been. Too late, too late.

I took a long time over my bath. It was hell getting into the thing and equally hell hauling oneself out but the bit in between was fine, more than could be said of the sight of myself reflected in the mirrored wall. A good deal of raw patches and blue and yellow bruising coming up all over the place. I wondered with a twinge of guilt if I'd be able to swing a club. God knows, it was dodgy enough anyway with a permanently dicky arm and, from the look of the bruising, I was due to stiffen up in no uncertain manner. Perhaps I should explain it to Chas.

I dried myself cautiously and asked myself why I hadn't already told him about being chucked out of the train. Come to that, I hadn't told anyone, not even the railway bodies, who certainly should have been informed of such goings on. With a back like mine I could hardly pretend that none of it had happened, but I knew perfectly well I was going to keep it to myself.

Down below, outside the open window, someone said, 'Three and two, Toby. Dinner's on me.'

I looked out into the gathering dusk. There was a golf green just beyond the courtyard and the last players of the day were coming in. From where I stood it seemed as though the whole of the island had been laid out as a golf course, and I suppose in a way it had. Chas had told me it was only a nine-hole affair, but on the other hand Sarne was not a big island. Seventy-five acres at the most, I guessed, of which the course would presumably take up about fifty. I wondered what it had cost Chas to lay it out. Something terrifying. But he was right about the castle, it made a good hotel, though with only about twenty rooms I couldn't see how he was going to get his money back. His problem, not mine. I stared down the first fairway to where the evening mist was starting to roll in from the sea. A few late gulls soared against the dull red sky, black-winged silhouettes screaming the end of the day. I put my jacket on and went down to see what she was like, this Kirstie Stewart Chas was planning to marry.

A good Scots name, Kirstie Stewart, and a bonny lass she turned out to be. I looked at her across the table at dinner and wondered what that solid tour golfer Chas MacLiven was going to pull out of the hat for his next trick.

He was pushing fifty, was Chas, and I gave Kirstie top whack at twenty-eight. Her hair was flaming red, her eyes green and if she wasn't strictly beautiful she had the kind of face that men remember with gratitude when they're old. She was wearing a long-sleeved shirt that matched her eyes and some kind of heavy costume jewellery round one wrist. Her voice still had a trace of native Scots in it and she had a trick of throwing her head back when she laughed. I couldn't take my eyes off her.

'Angus writes too,' Chas told her. It had just come out that she'd been some kind of journalist, which was where the 'too' came from.

'I know,' Kirstie said.

Chas looked impressed. 'You mean you've *read* his books?' You'd have thought that he personally never read anything much beyond *The Rules of Golf*.

She said coolly, 'Yes, they're very good.'

'Thank you,' I said.

'Chas said he'd a friend who was a policeman turned golfer. Now you write bestsellers too.'

'Golfer turned policeman,' I said.

'But you still play?'

'He damn well better,' Chas said, 'or he pays for his room.'

Kirstie said, 'I'm sure he wouldn't want to do that.' She was looking at me as she spoke and the hostility was too real to miss. Chas did, of course, but he had other things on his mind, but I got the message loud and clear. But why, for God's sake? Not all women like their men's friends but it should have been obvious that I wasn't going to lead Chas astray. I was no kind of competition, and I'd said nothing in the ten minutes since we'd met that could possibly be construed as treading on anybody's toes.

Chas said, 'You know something, Kirst? Angus calls the Donovans the same you do. The Heavenly Twins.'

Kirstie shook her head. 'What else?' Then to me, 'You came over with them?'

I nodded. 'They seemed obliging enough. A bit startling, I suppose, but all twins can't be little girls in matching dresses. What's wrong with them?'

'Every damn thing's wrong with them,' Chas said. 'They got no right hanging around here all the time.' He prodded the perfect smoked salmon on his plate. 'No right,' he said again. 'Back home we'd clear the brothers out, them and the rest of them.'

'If they're not breaking the law you can't turn them out,' Kirstie told him. 'Be reasonable, Chas. Even you know that.'

I said, 'They have friends?'

'I suppose you could call them that.' Kirstie might not have taken to me but she was prepared to go through the motions. 'It's an odd set-up but not really anything one can do much about. Have you ever heard of a man called Gavin Grant?'

I shook my head. 'No. Should I?'

'Not really, I suppose. He's a local oddity.' Kirstie frowned. 'Local liability too. He's in his seventies and years ago he was the Reverend Gavin Grant. Then apparently he had trouble with his health, couldn't remember things. In the end he retired while still quite a young man and settled down here.'

'What did he use for money?' I asked.

'He had money of his own,' Kirstie said. 'He has a place just outside Ardrossan with a good deal of land. Old Robbie MacLiven is supposed to have given him that—they were pretty close, I believe. He lived there as a sort of recluse until a few years ago. Until the Crofters came.'

'Real crofters?' But I knew they couldn't be. Crofters don't come, they are already there.

Kirstie shook her head. 'They're not real anything. It

started when some of those awful travelling people arrived —sort of middle-aged hippies left over from the 'sixties. All guitars and hash and filthy kids living in clapped-out cars. The kind of no-hopers who create a shambles at Stonehenge every year.'

'I know,' I said. 'Every policeman knows, because we have to move them on and the newspapers say we beat them up. So?'

'I don't honestly know.' Kirstie made a small gesture with hands that were slim and pale and had fingers about ten inches long. 'I don't *know*. They parked on Gavin Grant's land and got some hold over him. He said they were dispossessed and beloved of God, so the word got around and more and more travelling people arrived, till with Grant's help they formed what they call the Crofters' Community. They live on the old crofts and because Grant says they can stay nobody can turn them out, although they terrify the locals.'

'Do they really work the crofts?'

Kirstie laughed. 'Good Lord, no! They live on Social Security.' She paused. 'I'd forgotten about Stonehenge until now. Of course, that's where they got the idea from.'

'What idea?'

'Their *An Lataj Fearg*.'

It's a poor Scot who hasn't the Gaelic, and I hadn't. 'It's no good,' I said, 'you'll have to translate.'

Kirstie shrugged her shoulders. 'Literally, I suppose it means something like *The Day of Wrath*. It's the day of the highest tide of the year, so I suppose it's much like Midsummer's Day at Stonehenge. Way back, the locals celebrated it until the parsons said it was sinfully pagan. Now the Crofters have revived it.'

Strange, the appeal of Druid ritual for some people. Wrath and blood and slaughter stones, circles of the faithful praying to some personal fuzzy dawn. But it made a kind of sense: Midsummer's Day for farming folk, the high tide for fishermen. I asked, 'Where does the Wrath bit come in?'

'They say there's a freak tide every fifty years or so, when the winds and currents combine to make a sort of tidal wave. In the old days I suppose they sacrificed something —or someone—each year to avert it. As a matter of fact this year's *Lataj Fearg* ceremony comes up in a day or two. But no human sacrifice.'

I said, 'Chas should bill it as a local attraction.'

Kirstie threw back her head and laughed. 'He has! Transport laid on, picnic provided.'

'And where,' I asked, 'do the Heavenly Twins come in on all this?'

Kirstie frowned. 'I'm not absolutely sure whether they arrived with the others or joined them later, but they're— different. They're very thick with the Crofters, but there's no getting away from the fact that they're much brighter. They work pretty hard at diving and they've obviously got money, because that boat of theirs can't be cheap. But Chas hates them more than all the rest put together.'

I looked at him. 'Why so?'

'Hell, I don't know.' Chas shook his head impatiently. 'Forget it, Angus. Change the subject. Tell me what you think of Mistress MacLiven-to-be.'

'I think you've been wasting your time playing golf,' I said.

'So do I.'

'Tell me about the Pro-Am,' I said. 'Who's playing?'

'You and Gabriel Banda, Luther Koch and me.'

It sounded all right. Gabriel Banda was a brilliant black county cricketer whom I'd met once or twice in the past, a nice enough chap who played to a handicap of about four. Luther Koch was an up-and-coming West German professional. I said, 'I've met Gabriel, but I don't know a thing about Koch apart from what I've read.'

'Hits a ball a mile,' Chas said. 'Wrists like chrome steel with all that wheel-winding. He's a good guy, you'll like him.'

'That the lot?'

Chas looked hurt. 'It's the first one I've put on. Give it time to grow.'

We got through dinner amiably. It was a good meal, well cooked, perfectly served. We were drinking coffee when the barman came in and whispered that the television had packed up.

Chas shrugged his shoulders. 'Reception's lousy here, anyway. Get the guy over from Portree to fix it.' To me, 'Sorry about that. Anything you wanted to watch?'

'Do I look an addict?'

'You never can tell. They'll be lining up to complain tomorrow. You'd never believe how many folk come all the way up here to look at the box.' Chas brightened. 'Say, you wanted to see my ooblett!'

Ooblett. Oubliette. I was with it. 'Yes,' I said, 'I certainly did.' I didn't at that moment, I wanted to go to bed, but fair was fair.

Chas was happy again. 'You'll like it. It's pretty historical. Isn't it historical, Kirst?'

Kirstie said, 'I suppose so. I hate the damn place, but go ahead and show it him if you want to.'

'It's only kind of spooky because it's old.' Chas smiled at her affectionately. Since he was getting on for twice her age and she had the kind of looks that could stop a train, one might have expected him to be playing the part of the besotted dotard, but I doubt if Chas considered himself to be boxing out of his class. I think he was the kind of man who had always succeeded in doing whatever it was he'd set his mind to, and he'd achieved Kirstie in much the same way as he'd achieved his vast earnings from golf. He loved her and was proud of her, but the fact that he'd got her was nothing to do with luck. No sir. He'd got her because he was as good and in fact rather better than the next man and his girl had had the good sense to see this.

'You're right,' Kirstie told him, unsmiling. 'It's spooky and it's old. Go and show it off if you must. I'll see you later.'

'OK,' Chas said agreeably. He led the way out of the dining-room to the office behind the bar, muttering something about getting Miss Ailsa to take us.

'You mean you've got a guide?'

Chas didn't exactly look furtive but as near as he could get. 'Hell, no! She's what we call the housekeeper. You know, looks after the keys and such.'

'Single men and their housekeepers get into the Sunday papers,' I told him.

'Not this one doesn't,' Chas said, and I saw his point. Ailsa McCrae was one of those who could have been anything between forty-five and seventy, with a face remembered from a tapestry. All angles and unexpected planes. Her eyes were flinty blue, bleak and humourless, her scraped-back hair white, the kind of woman a sea rover might have had as a wife. She stood at the door of the office in a faded grey dress topped with an ancient knitted cardigan, and with some kind of nervous compulsion she plucked at one unravelled cuff with strong, spatulate fingers. I could see why Chas called her 'Miss Ailsa'. Probably her father had too.

'Mr Straun would like to see the dungeons,' Chas told her with a fine show of nonchalance. It was good to see the New World subdued by the Old for once. 'I thought maybe we could go right away.'

'If it's convenient,' I said, just to show Chas he wasn't the only one who could be humble.

'Aye.' Ailsa McCrae nodded to indicate that permission had been granted and felt in the pocket of that terrible cardigan before producing a formidable bunch of keys. 'Aye, we could go now if you wish it.'

'That's great,' Chas said. If he'd had a tail he'd have been wagging it hard as we followed Miss Ailsa. Behind the kitchens there was a flight of steps that wound down to what in my calculations must have been solid rock. Like everything else it had been cleaned up and well lit, but there was a chill about the place that came up and hit you.

I said, 'Is this one of your conducted tours?'

'They love it.'

I expect he was right, so why didn't I love it? Because Chas's guests were English and German and American and God knows what, and I was a Highlander? It's possible. I don't know, but race memory is an odd thing, and strange how the shades of fear and loneliness seemed to last through the years. Maybe some early Straun had ended up in a place like this, down in the dark and forgotten.

We came to the end of the stairs and came out into a kind of vault, perhaps thirty feet square, with a couple of open doorways through which one glimpsed a tiny space, raw stone and chains. I didn't doubt for a moment that the chains were as fake as the claymores upstairs in the hall. Surprising really that Chas hadn't got hold of a plastic skeleton to go with them, but it didn't take all that much imagination to dirty the place up and substitute some kind of smoking torch for the neatly wired electric light. Bad old days, they must have been. I wondered what perversity in my nature had prompted me to set my books in them when the tangible relics of the period never failed to give me the creeps.

'If you want to see the ooblett,' Chas said, 'it's over here.'

I'd seen the way into oubliettes before, like a covering to a well—which was really what those hellish prisons had been. As a prisoner you were lowered—or, for all I know, dropped—the twenty feet or so to the bottom, then the trapdoor was replaced and you were left down there in the dark. Presumably the jailers threw down food from time to time if it was required that the prisoner be kept alive, otherwise he died like a mouse in a bottle. I'd dug fairly deep to get my backgrounds right and it still made me uncomfortable to remember some of the things people used to do to each other five hundred years ago. What would it feel like to go mad in the dark, crawling around in your own filth with only the rats for company? Suddenly I knew that Kirstie was right and I shouldn't have come. Only that was ridiculous. It was because I'd wanted to see a well-preserved oubliette that I'd come up here in the first place, so I might as well get on with it.

'Right,' I said, 'let's have a look.'

Chas kicked the heavy wooden planks and they gave off a kind of hollow thud you used to get in Hammer films before the vampires came out. There was a handy iron ring and he gave it a heave. Hinges creaked, and the trap came up.

'Well now,' said the MacLiven, 'it's all yours.'

I took my look. It really was like looking into a well. Small, brick-sized blocks of quarried stone had been laid so as to form a six-feet-wide circular shaft from which a chill came up every bit as tangible as if you'd opened the lid of a freezer. The lights of the room in which we stood illuminated the first eight or ten feet of the oubliette but its lower depths were dark shadow. There were small grilles near the top that could have been windows, only they didn't look out anywhere.

'I thought we got lights fixed down there, so we could see the bottom,' Chas said.

'Longmore's man put them in a week past,' Ailsa McCrae told him. She walked to a switch on the wall. 'You had his account yesterday.'

Chas didn't say anything as she snapped the switch and well-covered halogen bulbs flooded the oubliette with stark white light. I looked down. The shadowless glare threw up the fresh pointing between the granite blocks, the yellow of lichen on the grey stone. It was a lot cleaner than it would have been in the old days. Then, as my eyes took in the bottom of the cell, fully twenty feet below me, I jumped. For a moment I honestly thought it was part of the show but then just as quickly I knew it wasn't.

'Oh Jeez—' Chas was saying.

There was a man down there at the bottom of the oubliette. He lay on his back, neatly dressed in pale blue slacks and a roll-neck sweater, his head at an odd angle, arms thrown wide. Even at a range of twenty feet he couldn't have looked more dead.

CHAPTER 5

'We'd better get him up,' I said at last. We'd been staring down at whoever it was for what seemed a long time without anyone saying anything at all. Corpses are great to chat about after a decent interval but tend to be inhibiting face to face.

'We'll need a ladder,' Chas said. He seemed to be finding it difficult to take his eyes off the sprawled thing below.

'And a rope,' I suggested. Oubliettes were fine to put people in but they weren't designed to get them out.

'Sure.' He kept staring down as though reluctant to leave. He looked past me to Ailsa McCrae. 'You know who that is? It's the guy from Room 1. Piet Werner.'

She nodded as though she'd known that already. 'The German.'

'South African,' Chas said. 'Afrikaaner.' He rubbed his

chin with the back of his hand. *By their habits you shall know them.* For years I'd watched him do just that while he wondered which club to take for a tricky one. He said, 'Great thing to happen to a guest,' and went to get rope and a ladder.

It wasn't funny getting Werner out. I went down to fix the rope round his shoulders and make sure he really was dead, though I should have been surprised if he'd been anything else with his head at that angle. Looking at him, it was easy enough to believe his name was Werner. Fair-haired, square face, bulky build. All very Nordic.

'You doing OK down there?' Chas asked from above.

I said yes. Shortish. I didn't mind Werner but I wish he'd chosen somewhere else to die, because being at the bottom of that well-like dungeon was bad enough in itself without having a genuine body in it with me. What's more, I'd discovered that the floor consisted of an iron grille through which I could smell the sea. Hygienically it must have had its advantages and, with any luck, the MacLiven prisoners must have died pretty smartly of cold, but it was a hellish place and I wanted out without any delay whatsoever.

I climbed up Chas's long aluminium ladder and between us we hauled the late Piet Werner out of his untimely grave. Chas had wanted to call up some help but Ailsa McCrae had stopped him and taken a share of the rope herself. She was a big, raw-boned woman but even so I was surprised at her strength. Werner came up heels first, his arms spread out like wings so that he cast grotesque shadows on the walls of his prison. They must have brought the dead up in the same way long ago. Flickering torchlight then, the creaking of a pulley wheel and the remains tidily dispatched over the cliff.

'Seems like he broke his neck.' Chas was not as moved as he might have been, which either meant he had little imagination or he'd seen a lot of men with broken necks before. I should have known which but I didn't.

I said, 'The neck's broken and the side of his head's crushed.' Then, when nobody made any comment, 'The coroner's going to say that he fell in and killed himself when he hit the bottom. And for once the coroner looks like being right. But, like the girl in the song, did he fall or was he pushed?'

Ailsa McCrae sniffed and plucked at her cuff. 'It's not occasion for laughter, Mr Straun, I'm thinking. But he was not being pushed when he met his end. He fell.' She was not one to beat about the bush, our Miss McCrae, oh dear no. I said, 'What makes you so sure?'

'Och, the poor man was for ever nosing about asking questions.' The way she put it, asking questions sounded unbelievably depraved. Also, she seemed to have no difficulty in suggesting that I did much the same.

I asked, 'Questions about what?'

Ailsa McCrae didn't shrug her shoulders because she wasn't that kind of woman, but if she had been she certainly would have done. 'About how the castle was made, and when, if you please. He'd a wee book he'd write notes in.' She paused. 'He didna think over much of the swords and suchlike in the hall.'

So it seemed that the late Mr Werner and I might have had something in common after all. 'You mean,' I said, 'that he was just interested in old buildings and weapons —that kind of thing?'

'Aye.' Miss Ailsa conveyed her feeling that she'd already made this clear. 'He said he'd been to just about every great castle in Europe and now he was starting on the small ones. He said that properly speaking this was no a castle at all, but it had some interesting features he wanted to have a good look at before they got spoiled.'

I heard Chas mutter something under his breath, but

there was something sticking out of the dead man's hip pocket and I bent down and pulled it out. It was an ordinary reporter's notebook with a spiral binding and when I flipped it open, you could see that the pages were filled with pencil sketches of cornerstones and battlements and buttresses, with accompanying notes in the kind of tiny rounded hand that seems to be as internationally a part of the architect's craft as is the doctor's carefully cultivated scrawl. What notes I read simply confirmed or enlarged on the drawings. The materials, dates, functions, presumed building techniques. I went through his wallet too but there was little of interest—credit cards, AvA membership—presumably a motoring club—money and a receipt or two. I put them back. Not my job, I was happy to say.

Chas glanced over my shoulder. 'Like Miss Ailsa says, some kind of military building nut. I guess he came back to have another look at the ooblett on his own and fell in. Easy enough to do—I nearly did it myself a couple of times.'

I said, 'That's great. Now suppose you tell me how our late lamented Mr Werner managed to shut the trapdoor after him.'

Miss McCrae looked at me. Chas looked at me. It was as though they'd joined together to applaud this example of the powers of detection.

'Hell!' Chas said at last. 'I shut the damn thing.' I waited for him to rub his chin, which he duly did. He went on, 'This morning. I sort of do a tour of the place after breakfast, just to see it hasn't fallen apart in the night. The trap was open, so I shut it.'

'Without looking inside?'

'I can't remember,' he said frankly. 'Maybe I glanced down, maybe I didn't. But one thing's for sure—the lights weren't on, so I wouldn't have seen the bottom whether I'd looked or not.'

Well, he was right about that, because I hadn't been able to see the bottom myself. But at least we'd had the thing shut to start with. 'It sounds bloody dangerous,' I said. 'Do you often find the trap's been left open?'

Chas scowled. 'Well, no. This was the first time. But you know how it is—we've had the workmen around and you're always falling over things. I didn't give it a second thought.'

I nodded, because after all, why should he? I said, 'We'd better ring the local police.'

'The phone's out of order.'

I'd forgotten, but he was right, because I hadn't been able to make a call from Skye. Phone out, television out. Come to the Golf Hotel for modern services. I asked, 'Did he come with a party?'

Chas shook his head. 'He was on his own. But he shared a table with another couple, so someone's going to ask where Werner's gone.'

'We'll leave him in one of the cells,' I said. 'See that no one comes down here till we get rid of him. But so far as the rest of the guests are concerned, you'll just have to tell them the truth.'

'Maybe we could say he'd died of a heart attack.'

'You could,' I agreed, 'but as the real story's going to come out at the inquest, there doesn't seem much point. You don't want your guests saying you've been trying to hush something up.'

Chas nodded. 'I guess you're right. You reckon the insurance will pay up if his relatives sue?'

I said, 'You'd better have a look at the small print. But if he was poking around on his own it could be his own fault.' The small print of an insurance policy doesn't usually make encouraging reading for anybody except the company but there didn't seem any point in making Chas more depressed than he was already.

'I'll look into it.' He turned to his housekeeper. 'That'll

be just fine, Miss Ailsa. Mr Straun and I will look after the rest.'

She said, 'I'll be away, then.'

It was interesting that Miss Ailsa knew when it was time for her to fall out. An excellent thing in a woman.

'You do that. This must have been a shock to you.' Chas managed a smile. 'Shock to all of us.'

Miss McCrae paused and fixed me with her pale blue stare. 'It's as well you had a strong wish to see the place, Mr Straun. Perhaps you've the sight.'

The sight. Memories of rather delicious excitements back in my childhood. Old Mistress Somebody or other who'd lived in a little stone cottage about a mile out of town. As small boys we'd spied on her and run like mad when she'd spotted us, which hardly made sense as nobody had ever suggested she'd the evil eye. But when my brother had got himself lost on the Cairngorms and the snow had come down, it had been Mistress Lewis who had told the search party where to go. She'd been right, too, although how does one know about a thing like that? It was a long time ago and the searchers might well have chosen that direction anyway, though I'd often wondered. 'I'd be a very surprised if I'd got the sight, Miss McCrae,' I said. 'I'm not even sure if I believe in it.'

'No?' She managed to let it be known that she was not altogether surprised. 'I was not here in those days, but folk say that Robbie MacLiven had it. The old laird, you understand.'

It was a good exit line.

Chas and I waited till she'd vanished round the first spiral of the stone steps, then got on with the business of depositing Werner's body in its provisional resting-place. After that we went up to Chas's office and had a large drink.

'Hell of a time for something like this to happen,' Chas observed.

I knew he was thinking of the Pro-Am and could hardly blame him, because corpses, accidental or otherwise, are not the stuff of good publicity. The last thing he wanted was to have police all over the place when his guests were supposed to be having a jolly, carefree time.

'Look,' I said, 'there's no problem. Koch and Banda are arriving tomorrow?'

Chas nodded. 'That gives them a day to settle in.'

'In which case we take Werner over first thing in the morning.' It sounded macabre, talking about the man as though he were still alive. 'Where's your nearest policeman?'

'Skye.' Chas frowned. 'You sure that'll be OK?'

'It's too dark to take him by boat now, and the phone's out of order.'

'I don't want to get in bad with the police.'

'For God's sake,' I said, 'I *am* the police.' Not strictly true, because I could imagine the reaction of the local coppers if a foreigner from south of the border tried to enter unasked into their affairs.

Chas nodded. 'Sure you are, I was forgetting. You couldn't do anything about those goddam hippies while you're about it, could you?'

'Afraid not,' I told him. 'It's really a local matter, you know. If there were enough complaints from people round here they might be able to do something about it, but it's not as though they were trespassing, because from what I hear, this fellow Grant *invited* them to stay.'

Chas stared into the bottom of his glass. 'He's not trying to run a hotel.'

I said comfortingly, 'Well, at least they're doing it all on shore. It's not as though they can get to your island.'

'You don't understand,' Chas told me. 'It's the look of the place. Everywhere you go ashore you find these weirdos hanging round. Not kids. Most of them must be *forty—*'

'It's by no means a unique phenomenon,' I said. 'People like that have a thing about Stonehenge.'

'But Stonehenge is a ruin or something, isn't it?'

'It's a ring of prehistoric standing stones near Salisbury,' I said. 'A cult place for leftover flower children. Go there on Midsummer's Day to watch the sun rise and get smashed on marijuana or what have you.'

Chas topped up my drink. We were sitting in his office with a bottle of malt between us and I made a note of the fact that we had been left on our own, which showed considerable restraint on Kirstie's part as she must have heard about the late Mr Werner by now. My host swallowed what he'd got in his glass and had some more. 'They're doing the same thing here. Our lot. The Crofters. Damn nearly everyone that's staying in the hotel is going off to watch it.'

'I know,' I said. 'The *Lataj Fearg*. The Day of Wrath. Kirstie told me about it.'

'They've dug out some local fairy tale. I've asked around but nobody seems to know what it's about.'

'But you're building it up as a big attraction.'

Chas grinned. 'Why not? I can't stop the bastards holding their shindig so I may as well build it up. You want to go?'

'No, thanks.' I shook my head. 'You know what happens?'

'Damn-all as far as I can make out. Except everyone gets drunk as a skunk. This place is lousy with superstition.'

A sudden blast of wind smashed against the side of the building. It didn't do the granite any harm but it shook the windows in their frames.

'Like your father having second sight?'

'Something like that.' Chas tilted the bottle again, ahead of me on this one. 'Not one hundred per cent stock-book parent, anyway. Adopted me when I was a kid.'

'I didn't know.' The embarrassment of the unasked-for

confidence about which there will be second thoughts in the morning.

'Och, I'm a good enough Scot. Guess I'm the old man's kid, anyway.' He caught my glance and grinned. 'The accepted theory is that I was washed ashore and oud Rabbie took me home and kept me. Would you believe it?'

'I don't know,' I confessed, 'but why not? You had to come from somewhere.'

'Don't kid yourself,' Chas said. 'If Rabbie found a kid washed up by the tide, fine. I guess he wouldn't throw it back. Sure, he'd find someone to look after it. But he sure as hell wouldn't adopt it *himself*.' He held up the bottle. 'You want another?'

I shook my head. I'd enough malt flowing through my bloodstream already and at least one of us was going to have to keep sober.

Chas swirled whisky round his glass. 'No,' he said finally, 'I guess oud Rabbie had got a bit above himself with one of the local girls. I reckon she dumped me on him and the old goat had to account for me somehow, so he made out he'd found me on the beach.' He swallowed reflectively. 'So it makes a change from underneath a gooseberry bush.'

We all believe what we want to believe. I could think of several good reasons why I personally found it difficult to see oud Rabbie as an embarrassed father or, for that matter, as a kind of beachcomber. I put the problem aside and said, 'It's been a long day.'

'Sure has.' Chas roused himself. 'One for the road?'

'You'd better turn in too.'

Chas said, 'You're right,' but he didn't move, so I left him to it and went on upstairs. Half way up I met cosy Mr Meuse coming down and he said good night to me in what seemed to be his usual mild way. I wondered if he'd got a wife with him or if he was alone in the hotel, but by that time he'd passed and gone out of my mind because I'd reached my room and was fumbling for the key.

It was an effort to force myself to undress and get into bed. The curtains were drawn back so that the moon shone through the open window like a street lamp and I could hear the surf beating at the bottom of the cliff a hundred feet straight down, a dull background growl that was probably pleasant enough in daylight but made me restless in the dark. I knew now that I wished I hadn't accepted Chas's invitation in the first place, but it was clearly too late to back out. But what had I got myself into?

Nothing, logic answered back at me. You've got yourself into nothing except a little golf and the company of an amiable and hospitable host. The fact that an unknown young man called Piet Werner has had the misfortune to fall and break his neck is nothing to do with you. Nor does it matter that Chas MacLiven's very personable girlfriend clearly wishes that you would go away. Do you expect every woman you meet to like you instantly? Isn't it conceivable that you have offended her in some way?

Like the man on the train.

I was tired of thinking about the train but it was difficult to stop, because after all you have to drop a hell of a big brick before someone tries to kill you. So it could have been an accident. But common sense said oh no, it couldn't. If that door had opened accidentally the chap behind me would have pulled the emergency thing and stopped the train, whereas as I very well knew, the thing had rolled on merrily to Fort William.

No, I thought, the whole thing had got a bad feel about it. Perhaps that meant I had the sight like randy oud Rabbie. I laughed as I closed my eyes but I was alone in the big bed and there was no one to laugh with me.

CHAPTER 6

The policeman who met us at Ardrossan was much as Chas had described him, a dour laddie, raw-boned and in sight of his pension, but he helped to get Werner out of the helicopter handily enough.

'The poor gentleman,' he said. 'It's a sad thing, the accidents they're always having. He fell, you say?' The compassion of hard men, curiously touching.

'It seems likely,' I said.

Chas and I had smuggled Werner's body out of the hotel and into the chopper before guests were up and about, discretion being the hotelier's stock in trade.

McDonald nodded. Taking into account the number of lunatic climbers who visited the area each year, he was probably more used to people killing themselves than one might think and at least he'd brought a plain van with him. We stowed the body away in it and shut the door.

McDonald eyed me speculatively. 'You'll be dealing with this further, sir?'

I wondered where he'd picked up my particulars and hoped nowhere official. 'I shall not,' I told him. 'This is not my patch, McDonald, and I've no doubt your Super would say the same.'

He smiled faintly. 'Aye.'

'Has anyone said when the inquest is likely to be?'

'Dr Cameron has a liking for Tuesdays,' McDonald said.

I nodded. I very nearly said something about getting in touch with South Africa House but changed my mind. Chas had already told the police at Fort William that he had no record of the dead man's next of kin and they weren't going to thank me for any suggestion of mine that looked as though it might be telling them what to do. I was here to play golf, after all, and that didn't include poking my nose into another force's business.

'Christ,' Chas said. 'We forgot the poor bastard's luggage.' He went back to the chopper and came back carrying a suitcase and an airline bag, a camera and a lightweight raincoat.

'He'll not be needing them, I fancy,' McDonald commented, 'but it's best you're shot of them.' He stowed them away beside their erstwhile owner and somehow his worldly goods made him look deader, if possible, than he had been before. The van went off down the street to await the ferry, leaving Chas and me staring after it. A squad of quarrelling seagulls screamed over our heads, dazzling white against a sky that was suddenly bluer than it had been since I arrived. We both stared at the neat grey houses and the sober police van growing smaller between them, and at least half of us wondered what Piet Werner had been planning to do today. Probably a stimulating appointment with a flying buttress. Oh, very funny. What made me so convinced that I wasn't going to be rolled up in a blanket in the back of a plain van in twelve hours' time?

Chas said, 'Haven't flown that kind of freight since Viet Nam.'

'You haven't lost your touch,' I told him. So that was where he'd learned to fly a helicopter. I hadn't even known that Chas had been in Viet Nam. Why hadn't I known?

'Like riding a bicycle, I guess. One body bag's pretty much like another. You don't forget.' He turned away. 'Let's go get us a drink.'

The West Highland was the nearest, so we went to that. There was a girl in a leather jacket sitting at the bar with her back to the door, with red hair spilling over the collar. Women still don't sit at bars in the Highlands and I was surprised that they'd let her get away with it, but then

Kirstie didn't strike me as the kind of girl you pushed around lightly.

She said, 'Hi!'

'Hi!' Chas settled himself beside her as though the meeting was not a surprise. 'She took the boat,' he explained to me. 'She's working on a story.' Such of Chas's reading that I'd noticed had been rather up-market. It would be an exaggeration to say that he now spoke of a little local journalism with awe but there was certainly respect. Well, why not indeed?

I asked her what story.

'Newcomers to the island,' she told me. 'You wouldn't believe it, but there's an ex-bank manager from Purley translating local folk songs from the Gaelic.'

'I believe it,' I said. 'Where's all this coming out?'

'The *Western Chronicle*.' She said that without apologies, and bully for her. She didn't say 'a local rag, but next year I'll be on a London daily', but I got the impression that was what she meant. In which case, how did that tie up with marriage to Chas?'

I said, 'I'll look out for it. What are you drinking!'

'Whisky.'

The man behind the bar served us with good grace and we chatted amiably, until Chas put his glass down and turned for the door.

'I gotta go,' he announced. 'Got a date with the bank, so I'll see you back here in a couple of hours.' He glanced in my direction. 'How about it, Angus? Want a trip to Fort William or you staying to look after Kirstie for me?'

Put like that, it was lucky I didn't particularly want to go to Fort William. 'I'll stay,' I said.

'Just as you like. You OK, Kirst?'

'Yes, darling, I'm fine.'

Yes, darling, I'm fine. The last thing she wanted was to be looked after by me but Chas had got us both in positions from which it would be hard to duck out of without actually being rude.

'See you, then.' Through the window we watched him walk over to where the Westland was parked on the school playing field. He climbed into his little plastic bubble, the rotors sighed and turned and then he was clattering away, dwindling in size against the sky like some ungainly grass-hopper till he vanished behind the rim of the hills.

'Do you suppose,' I said, 'one can make a phone call?'

She nodded over my left shoulder. 'One can. Just past the palm tree in a pot. It says *Telephone*.' Her voice now included dislike for foreigners who condescended to the Highlands by assuming they might not have telephones. I was a Scot too, damn it. And I was only making the call to give her the chance to get away. Well, not entirely.

I located the thing and dialled Laurie's number. By rights she should have been in Ireland but at least I'd go through the motions. Her 'phone rang twice and then she answered.

'I thought you would have gone to Ireland.' There should have been another way of putting it, and the telephone only seems to give you one chance.

'I'm going tonight.' Then, 'How's your oubliette?'

'All right,' I said. 'There was a body in it.'

'What do you mean, there was a body in it? You mean a waxwork or something?'

'No,' I said, 'it wasn't a waxwork. A dead body. Appar-ently someone fell in.'

'An accident?'

'So far as one can tell.'

'Oh.' There was a pause while the line crackled and she thought it over. Or at least that's what I thought she was doing, although when she spoke again she was off at a tangent.

'Angus, you remember the antique dealer you told me about—the one who steals cannon balls?'

'Smith,' I said. 'Of Sommerton Row. What's he got to do with my body?'

'He hasn't anything to do with it, this is something different.' She paused. 'Are you listening?'

'Yes,' I said.

'Well, I went there.'

'I bet he wasn't open.'

'Oh yes, he was.' I could hear her satisfaction in the flat denial. 'I went in and asked him if he'd got any cannon balls.'

God, I thought, I bet that surprised him. Surprised me too, come to that. 'All right,' I said, 'I'll buy it. Did he have any?'

'No, he didn't.'

I wasn't all that surprised, because I'd always imagined that for kleptomaniacs the act of pinching was all, but there were presumably degrees of nuttiness. Perhaps Smith had a secret museum of Tudor hardware hidden away under his shop where he could count it or something.

Laurie was presumably thinking along the same lines, because her voice said in my ear, 'Maybe he has a client who likes cannon balls and he gets them on his behalf.'

'It's possible,' I agreed. 'But in that case, why doesn't he just buy what he wants?'

'To save money, I suppose.' Then as the thought struck me, 'Did he ask you what you wanted a cannon ball *for*?'

'Yes,' she said. 'He did, as a matter of fact. I told him my father wanted one to use as a doorstop.'

You'd have to be crazy to use a sphere for a door stop, I thought, but off the cuff it wasn't bad. I said, 'I can't pretend to understand it, but thanks anyway.'

'That's all right.' It was a pointless sort of conversation, but then the telephone is always bad at the kind of chat when you need to see the other person. It was a relief when the thing wanted more money and I'd run out of change.

'Must go. Ring when I get back.'

'Goodbye.'

I went back to the bar, conscious of the fact that if anything, I'd made things worse rather than better. To my surprise, Kirstie was still there.

'Get through?'

'Yes, thanks, fine.'

We started to walk along the edge of the quay. The wind had dropped and the water was virtually flat within the shelter of the sea wall, and you could see the odd beer can poking up out of the sand, amphora of the twentieth century. A couple of trawlers were nosing their way in from a trip and a screaming plume of gulls were doing their best to strip whatever the catch was off their decks.

I made conversation. 'Who are you interviewing this morning?'

'A couple who've started making fishing-rods.'

'You could probably get some quite good stuff out of the guests at the hotel.'

Kirstie laughed for the first time. 'You're right. As a matter of fact, I'm covering your Pro-Am match. At least, I'm taking the pictures. I don't really know a great deal about golf.' She had a cased camera slung over her shoulder, the leather scuffed enough to show it was no toy.

I said, 'You should get that chap Meuse to help out.'

'Oh, Mr Mouse! He's sweet, isn't he?' Mr Mouse. Ridiculous name but not inappropriate. Then she said, 'Why him?'

'He seems deeply into photography.'

'Is he? I hadn't noticed.' Kirstie had been watching the gulls harrying the trawler, now she switched back to me, green eyes wary. 'Come on, Straun, you're fishing for something. What do you want to know?'

I said, 'I'd like to know what I've done to put your back up. You've been waiting to sink your teeth into me from the minute we met.'

A gust of wind blew a strand of that incredible hair across her eyes and she tossed her head impatiently. 'Don't be ridiculous. We've never met, so what could I possibly have against you?'

If I'd known I wouldn't have been asking, but I said, 'The classic reason would be because you thought I'd come between you and Chas.'

She stopped and faced me. She wasn't angry, but I suspected that if at that moment I'd dropped dead at her feet she wouldn't have shed many tears.

'And why,' she asked, 'would you want to do that?'

I shrugged my shoulders. 'Chas is an old friend. Maybe someone should tell him his girl works for the KGB.'

'I *don't* work for the—' She broke off abruptly. 'Damn you, Straun, just play your game and go home.'

'Look,' I said, 'it would save a lot of time if you'd tell me what the trouble is.'

'No trouble. There isn't any, so forget it.' We stood facing each other for a moment and then she laughed. 'I'm sorry,' she said. 'I really have been rude.' She took my arm impulsively and towed me along the quay. 'Tell me who you were ringing just now. Your wife? No, Chas says you haven't got a wife. But you've got somebody, because—'

I can't imagine that she dried up because she was embarrassed, far more likely because she'd realized I was barely listening to her. The Heavenly Twins' Sea Chief was moored at the far end of the quay and a small group of holidaymakers and Crofters were staring down at something Sean and Patrick had presumably just brought ashore. I glimpsed the two of them on deck, lifting something heavy.

'Seems they've brought something up,' Kirstie said.

We walked over. There was the strange, wet smell in the air that you notice when something's been at the sea bottom a long time, but at first we couldn't see anything but people. Directly in front of me a middle-aged man in shorts and a

Fair Isle sweater was squinting through the viewfinder of his camera and talking to no one in particular.

'Funny to think that stuff's been down there since the Spanish Armada.'

I edged past him. What lay on the granite had been a culverin. Parts of it were defaced by rust and much of the rest was covered with a growth of barnacle-like shellfish but the general shape of the weapon showed through well enough. The mouth of the barrel was clear and, not for the first time, I found myself wondering how it could ever have been worthwhile to mount and man a popgun that fired a projectile not much bigger than a pingpong ball. The thing had been too small even to have wheels—it was still possible to identify the metal post beneath the barrel that had dropped into some kind of deck mounting. But the culverin's qualities as a weapon were really secondary to the thing's existence. It was a popgun from the fifteen-hundreds, lost for four centuries and lying here in front of me. Beside it there were a couple of roughly circular objects that I guessed to be pewter plates, something that could have been a link of chain.

'It's stuff from the *Santa Marina*,' the man in shorts was saying. 'Spanish Armada and all that. Those two lads have been diving for it.'

A woman's voice said, 'I suppose that round thing's a cannon ball.'

I hadn't seen the round thing but it was there all right, hidden behind a bollard. On an impulse I went over and picked it up, an eight-pounder, I guessed. Still wet from the sea as I turned it over.

Kirstie touched my arm. 'What's the matter?'

'Nothing.' It was just an ordinary cannon ball, its surface dull with the patina of age and fragments of ancient shell. There could hardly have been anything more transparently genuine, so it was sheer bloody-mindedness on my part to admit to being the smallest bit disappointed.

CHAPTER 7

'I must be going,' Kirstie was saying. 'My fishing-rod couple will be waiting.'

I put the cannon ball back and straightened up. Behind me, cameras were still clicking and the visitors were making appropriate noises to show they were impressed.

'Straun—'

'I know,' I said, 'your fishing-rod people are waiting. I'll see you back at the hotel, with Chas.' Then a thought struck me. 'Look, you know this place. Has it got a museum—a local historian or something?'

'To tell you about cannon balls?'

I could have sworn my face hadn't changed when I'd seen the thing, but even quite dim women can be clairvoyant at times.

I said, 'Shipwrecks in general, the Armada in particular. There's usually some dedicated enthusiast who's worth meeting.'

Kirstie bit her lip. For a moment I got the feeling she was toying with the idea of just not knowing, but the place was a bit small for that.

In London it would have taken me months to find whoever it was, but here on Skye she must have known that if she didn't tell me, someone else would.

Finally she said, 'Gavin Grant. He's quite a well-known Gaelic scholar and he's always had a personal thing about the Armada.'

We'd moved away from the group admiring the Heavenly Twins' treasure trove, but we had to step aside to let a particularly noisome party of beaded and bearded misfits drift past. All the men were approaching middle age, the wan drabs who accompanied them were just studies of timeless despair. I nodded towards them. 'You mean *that* Gavin Grant?'‘

'That Gavin Grant.'

There was no reason why the king of the hippies should not be an Armada scholar but it seemed unusual. But this was Kirstie's home ground, not mine. 'Where do I find him?' I asked.

She gestured to the south. 'He has a thing about walking along the cliff in the mornings.' She narrowed her eyes. 'You can see him now, as a matter of fact. Look.'

I looked. Two figures, tiny against the backdrop of the hills. 'Who's the other one?'

'His—' She stopped and started again. 'He likes to have one of his friends with him.'

'His minder?'

On one of the fishing-boats a man emptied a bucket overboard and the waiting seagulls screamed and pounced. It made the sort of picture you could have sold to the Scottish Tourist Board, all white wings against blue sky. Come to the Highlands and forget your troubles.

Kirstie turned her green eyes on me and, when she spoke, her voice was little above a whisper. 'Oh, Straun! Why don't you just *go*?'

I caught up with Gavin Grant half a mile out of town, a tall, thin, white-haired figure in a fisherman's jersey and an ancient deerstalker, leaning against an outcrop of granite and scanning the horizon through a pair of ex-Navy binoculars. He lowered the binoculars as I approached him and I saw that he had the long, lean face that they used to give to martyrs on mediæval frescoes, but without the mad eyes. Gavin Grant's were grey and curiously childlike and when he smiled I felt he'd been looking forward to meeting me for a long time.

I introduced myself and said, 'I was wondering if we might have a talk about what happened to the Armada ships in these parts. I gather you're something of an authority.'

Grant's companion said, 'He knows it all, man.'

Grant's companion was florid and bearded and wore a dirty T-shirt and tattered jeans. He had beads round his neck and sandals on muddy feet. He was about my age and his speech sounded as dated as if he'd been wearing Air Force uniform and spoke of wizard prangs. Also his teeth were bad and the whites of his eyes pink. Oh dear. I pictured him with a name like Beastly Basil, and I was spot on.

Gavin Grant smiled shyly. 'I'm afraid Basil exaggerates. Sir Julian Corbett's an authority. So is Van der Essen. And, come to that, J. A. W. Williamson's *Hawkins of Plymouth* is a very considerable book. I've not written a word, you understand.' The cultured, slightly pedantic tones of the well-universitied academic overlaying the lilt of an earlier dialect. He added, 'And you?'

'I suppose,' I said, 'I'm just a seeker after knowledge.'

'Like the lama. A lovely book.' He lowered himself on to a convenient lump of rock and gestured to me to join him. 'I assume you require knowledge of the Armada. Some particular knowledge?'

I said, 'I was wondering if you could tell me something about the *Santa Marina*.'

'Ah.' I don't suppose he was surprised because in the circumstances it was a fairly obvious question. He stared down at his binoculars and fiddled with them. Then he said, 'She was a twenty-four gun two-decker, a little under three hundred tons. Probably carried some demi-culverins as well, though one can never be sure about these things. They had the same range as a full culverin, you understand, but threw a nine-pound ball instead of eighteen. Her commander was a Captain Juan de Souza and he carried a hundred fighting men with him, which was a fine load to carry for a fighting ship, particularly when the weather became rough.'

'*God blew and they were scattered.*'

The old man frowned. 'My dear sir, you must realize that there's an immense amount of nonsense talked about Armada galleons and storms. I grant you that there was a wind that blew at gale force from August 20th, if my memory serves me in the matter. But the Spaniards were beaten before that. Before they set sail, even.'

There is always something about the true enthusiast that carries conviction, even when wrong. So I asked, 'Why was that, Mr Grant?'

He looked up from his binoculars and said mildly, 'One can only imagine they had offended God in some way, and their chastisement was inevitable. Of course it is marvellous the manner in which God can make drunkards and lechers the chosen instruments of His will.'

I said tentatively, 'You mean Drake—'

'No, Mr Straun, I do not mean Drake.' Gavin Grant made a gesture of irritation. 'One hears so much about Drake and his little ships harrying the Armada, but of course that is in no way the truth. Our ships were as large or larger than those of the enemy and they had guns to match. They could outmanœuvre the Spaniards, not because they were small but because Hawkins had built ships without top-heavy fighting castles at each end, and he'd decked in the midships to make an extra gun platform. The Lord had willed that the ships of Spain be outclassed, d'you see?'

'Yes,' I said, 'I do see.' I wasn't sure which side he was on but I followed him all right.

Gavin Grant stared out to sea as though he was watching it all. He said slowly, 'The Armada galleons weren't packed with guns, they were packed with men. Soldiers, who were supposed to board the English fleet, only of course they never had the chance, they just stood there while their ships were pounded at long range. By the time the Armada broke away and fled north it was a beaten rabble—'

It was time to get Gavin Grant back on course, too. 'So what happened to the *Santa Marina*?' I asked.

'Oh, she went north with the rest.' The old man shrugged his frail shoulders. His eyes weren't on me, they stared past me as though he was watching some kind of war game, which for all I know he was. He said, 'She'd lost some rigging and her crew had a hard time getting round the Wash and the cavaliers had to throw their horses overboard. In the end she went north of the Orkneys and hugged the west coast of Scotland, heading for Ireland. By that time she was falling to pieces. So much so that according to some accounts her captain had to lower a hawser beneath the keel so that he could tie his ship together like a parcel.' He paused.

'And in the end?' I prompted.

Beastly Basil had been lying stretched out on the grass, apparently asleep, but now he opened his eyes and sat up. He said, 'In the end the bloody thing sank anyway. Just off the Old Quay.' He looked at Gavin Grant. 'That right, man?'

The old man picked up his glasses again. 'Yes, that's right.'

The three of us were staring out to sea now. God knows what we thought we were looking at, we must have looked like something out of a Becket play. Finally Grant asked, 'Are you the Straun who used to play a lot of golf?'

It wasn't what I'd expected him to say, but not unflattering. 'I expect so,' I told him.

'We have a nice little course a couple of miles from here.' Grant gave me another of those shy smiles of his. He could be an appealing old chap. 'It would be a privilege to play a few holes with you before you go. I'd enjoy it so much.'

'You're very kind.' I thought it extraordinarily unlikely
that I was going to have time for any such thing, but it was
hard to hand out a flat refusal, so I said lamely, 'I'm afraid
I'm rather committed—'

Beastly Basil scratched his chest and shook his head at
Grant. 'Out of your class, man.'

'I'm a guest of Mr MacLiven so my movements rather
depend on him.' I'd only known Beastly Basil for a few
minutes and I could cheerfully have pushed him off the cliff.
Now what had possessed Grant to harbour him? To give a
home to any of them, for that matter? But of course, I didn't
know. If I'd known the way his mind worked, I wouldn't
have considered him mildly dotty in the first place. 'Look,'
I said, pointedly ignoring Basil, 'I'd very much enjoy a
game with you. Would it be all right if I saw how I'm fixed
and let you know?'

'My dear fellow, that would be splendid!' Gavin Grant's
ascetic face lit up. 'I shall look forward to it so much.'

I think he was going to say something else but Basil
looked at his watch and got up hurriedly. 'Time we were
going, squire.'

'Is it?' Gavin Grant rose obediently. To me he said, 'A
pleasure to meet you, Mr Straun. I do hope—'

'Yes,' I told him, 'so do I.' And in an odd way I meant
it.

They looked an odd couple as they began their walk back
towards the little town and I didn't follow them right away.
Instead I sat down on the grass and looked out over the
little harbour and beyond to the old, broken quay that
nobody used any more. Somewhere off there was where the
Santa Marina had gone down, the spot where the Donovan
twins claimed they were already finding what was left of the
old ship.

In the end the bloody thing sank, anyway was what Basil had
said. And Gavin Grant had agreed.

I picked up a stone and tossed it over the edge of the cliff. It struck a rock and skidded off into the waves, while the gull that had dived hopefully after it changed its mind and soared on out to sea. I was prepared to believe that Gavin Grant knew more about the Armada than I did, because he'd probably been studying it for most of his adult life. Like students of Waterloo or those Americans who constantly refight the war between the States, he'd know who made the commanders' shirts and the colour of their mistresses' eyes.

Well, I couldn't compete with that—a plain copper who wrote historical novels in his spare time. On the other hand, I was a plain copper who was half way through writing a book set in the England of 1588 and I'd researched the Armada pretty well, and one thing that research had taught me was that the *Santa Marina* was no insignificant, run of the mill galleon. On the contrary, she was one of the Captain General's Great Ships, and one which had accomplished the well-nigh impossible. She never foundered off the coast of Scotland. Falling apart she may have been, but according to the official records of the time, the *Santa Marina* actually made it back to Spain.

CHAPTER 8

Once a man conceives an idea that is ill-advised, fate usually falls over itself to help him develop it fully. I was curious about the Heavenly Twins and their diving project, suspecting it as a piece of mildish villainy, although not sure what. They could have been a couple of darlin' Irish boys having a bit of healthy fun. It was possible they were playing fast and loose with the rules of Treasure Trove but my personal money was on an excise fiddle of some kind. But the Western

Isles were a long way off my patch and no self-respecting copper was going to thank me for pushing my nose into what was rightly his.

But of course fate, in the person of Chas MacLiven, fixed all that.

Four of us had walked the course after dinner, Kirstie, Chas, Gabriel Banda and myself. Chas's idea, and why not? Riders walk the Grand National, tournament golfers study an unfamiliar course in order to get the general feel of the place and reflect on the angles of the greens. To walk a hotel's amenity nine-holer may have been giving the place ideas above its station, but Chas was my host and it was a pleasant evening, so what harm in a little gentle exercise?

Chas's pride and joy wasn't exactly a model of mature elegance, but experience and money had produced nine very fair holes. The fairways were of that marvellous Highland turf that never seems to need cutting, wide enough but adequately bunkered. In places one was required to drive rather hair-raisingly along the cliff edge in a way that might be expected to scare even the most determined slicer into a hook, but it was straightforward and fun and, for anyone who played even fair golf, not exactly anything to worry about.

We'd passed a little huddle of stone cottages standing on the side of the third green and a couple of women wearing traditional shawls had paused at the doors of their homes to watch us go by. Kirstie had smiled at them but got nothing in return. It seemed more than the usual distrust of the stranger, but I could have been mistaken.

Later, in the bar, Banda had asked what the natives of Sarne did for a living.

Chas said shortly, 'Damn few do anything. The kids don't fancy the simple life any more, so soon as they're old enough to hold down a job, they quit and head for the mainland.

Half of them don't get a job there either, but they still don't come back.'

'And in the good old days?' It was always a surprise to find that Gabriel Banda's wonderful deep brown voice spoke the very best English English.

'Lot of shark fishing.'

'Shark?'

'Sure, lot of oil in a shark's liver, they tell me.' Chas sounded proud of the sharks.

Banda looked suitably impressed. 'So what happened to the business? Nobody want shark liver oil any more?'

'Hell, I don't know.' Chas corrected himself. 'Don't know about the oil, know about the business, though. The fishermen used to live in cottages down the bottom of the cliff till high tides washed them out. They tried again from one of the other islands but the sharks weren't around any more. It happens. One of those things.'

I asked, 'Did they ever come back?'

'Nope.' Chas shook his head. 'Small ones now and then, that's all. Not that their livers are in demand any more, because they're not.' He seemed lost in a world that was a sad place without sharks. But he made an effort and saw the best of it. 'At least we can rent out our scuba gear.'

Scuba gear. I felt the finger of fate touch my shoulder. I must have radiated the word or something, because Chas looked across at me. 'What's with it, son? You want to dive?'

It was a long time since I'd put on a wetsuit. As is probably the case with most claustrophobics, there are bits and pieces about diving that I don't take to, like going inside caves and the darker parts of wrecks, the things you don't particularly think about afterwards, balanced by the ones you do. I'd done a course in the way of business and then gone on to learn a bit more for fun. Now, facing Chas's question, I wasn't sure whether I wanted to dive or not but

I did know I wanted to have a look at the Donovans' wreck.

'Great!' I said. 'Why not?' Never had a host a more appreciative guest.

I waited for my round of applause but in vain. In the little moment of silence Kirstie said, 'For goodness sake, Straun! Don't be an idiot!'

'Now look, Princess,' Chas objected amiably, 'let the man dive if he wants to.'

'You want another guest to kill himself?'

Chas frowned and I guessed that he didn't exactly welcome chat on that subject in open bar. If a guest has an unfortunate accident and breaks his neck, it's not a thing one hushes up, but on the other hand one tries not to make it a talking point in public. He said shortly, 'Why in hell should the man kill himself?'

'He doesn't know the water round here.' Kirstie must have known it was a waste of time arguing on those grounds. Chas had made his home in Florida for goodness knows how many years, among a people who breathed pressurized air as a matter of course. To make a fuss about someone going diving was roughly on a par with calling a bicycle a deathtrap. She looked at me with something in those green eyes that could have been an appeal, but I wasn't looking too hard. 'You really want to go?'

'Yes,' I said politely. 'If it isn't too much trouble.'

'OK, Straun,' she said, 'I'll come with you.'

Chas looked at me apologetically. 'The Princess gets to fussing at times.' He tossed her a crumb of caution. 'Better switch on the TV and check on the weather.'

Kirstie shook her head. 'Can't—it's on the blink again.'

'Jesus!' Chas checked himself politely in case he said something offensive about the Brits and their place in the twentieth century. I imagined he was remembering that in Florida, not only did everyone dive efficiently but also the mechanics of life worked one hundred per cent. He said with some restraint, 'It'll be in the paper. And see if you can get someone to fix that set tomorrow latest.'

Kirstie got up and went in search of a paper while we waited. Personally I wasn't over-worried about the weather which, apart from the odd patch of mist, seemed settled enough, but one was conscious of a certain digging in of heels. When she came back she said, 'No paper.'

'What d'you *mean*—"no paper"?' Chas's voice had taken on a querulous note, unusual for him. 'Who are you fooling, Kirst? There are *three* papers!'

'Well, there may have been,' Kirstie told him, 'but there aren't now.'

'But where *are* they?'

I said helpfully, 'Forget it, Chas. It's the end of the day. Either the guests have nicked them or they've been thrown away.'

'Miss Ailsa!'

The housekeeper was in the office, fortunately only yards away. She came but, I thought, with disapproval.

'Mr Straun is going diving in the morning,' Chas told her, 'and we need a weather forecast. Have you collected today's papers and thrown them in the garbage or something?'

Miss Ailsa plucked at her cardigan, presumably to indicate irritation. She said bleakly, 'No, Mr MacLiven, I have not.'

'Then where—'

'The guests may be taking them. But not I.'

I caught her eye. 'It's all right, Miss McCrae,' I said hastily, 'I can get it on the radio in my room.'

'Thank you, Mr Straun.' Thanks be that there is one gentleman here. Then to Chas, 'Will that be all, then?'

He could have laughed, but he didn't. It was a new Chas, this worried man. 'That's all, Miss Ailsa. Sorry to have troubled you.'

She said, 'It's no trouble,' and took herself off.

We all took ourselves off, Chas and Kirstie together, Gabriel Banda and I to the paving by the first green. If we had lived in the good, brave days when one could smoke without getting neurotic about it, we'd have enjoyed a last cigarette. The moon was up, almost full, and in its light the castle of the MacLivens looked much as it must have done a good many centuries ago. I said as much and Banda laughed.

'No cars.' He gestured to the empty space in front of us. Chas's chopper was round the corner, out of sight. 'Take the cars away, it always makes a difference.'

He was right, of course. It wasn't worth while for guests to bring cars to a tiny island, they left them parked at Mallaig, on the mainland. I remembered asking Chas if Werner had a parked car we should be taking care of, and his answer had been definite.

'No car. Werner was wild for the good old days, that's why he was such a nut about castles. Told me himself he couldn't drive.'

I remembered leafing through the dead man's pocket book, the membership cards for this and that. A card with AvA. Why should a man who couldn't drive be a member of a motoring association? I stopped myself there, rather glad I wasn't thinking out loud.

I turned to Gabriel. '*Is* there an Automobile Association in South Africa? The AvA?'

If he was surprised he didn't show it. 'There's the AA.'

I remembered Werner's membership card. 'No,' I said, 'AvA.'

Gabriel Banda looked at me. He was pretty black and in the half light his eyes seemed twice as big. He said gently, 'You pulling my leg, man?'

'I'm pulling nobody's leg. It's just something I want to know.'

He nodded, as though I'd cleared up a point that had been bothering him. 'As a matter of fact, there is an AvA, but it's nothing to do with cars. It stands for Afrika voor Afrikaaners. Strong right-wing pro-apartheid stuff. You thinking of joining?'

'No,' I told him. 'The only chap who'd have got me in just died.'

Gabriel smiled. 'Well, it wasn't me who did it.' He got up. 'Got to get my sleep. Good night, Inspector.'

Good night, ladies. Good night. Good night.

I watched him go. I wished I'd thought of that AA business earlier, but I couldn't see what difference it made. So Piet Werner had been some kind of fundamentalist Boer, but it didn't exactly follow that a well-known Liberal black sportsman would murder him on sight. A cat wailed somewhere and reminded me I was due for a little scavenging on my own, so I stood up and headed in the direction of where I imagined the kitchens would be. The lights were still on but I was in no mood to hang about all night waiting for the washing up staff to go to bed. I'd seen myself taking the covers off dustbins rather like a chef inspecting his wares, but, in the event, it wasn't necessary because close to the kitchen door there was a pile of old newspapers weighed down with a brick. I walked up casually and helped myself to the top one and bore it off to my room.

The *Western Chronicle*. Today's date. So Ailsa McCrae *had* gathered them up and dumped them! I was amused that she had outfaced Chas's transatlantic aggression with such aplomb. I turned to the back page, reserved for football results and television programmes. Somebody had rested a wine glass on a goalkeeper's head and given him a pink halo but otherwise it was all there. I looked at the television programmes, and it didn't take long for me to find what I was looking for, because, just in case I should miss it, there was a picture of a Mr Aaron Abrahams looking out at me, with a caption stating that he could be seen in interview on BBC2 at 8.30 p.m. I looked at it for some time. The mild, intelligent face was familiar all right, although not as Aaron Abrahams. So far as I was concerned, the chap in the picture was Kirstie's favourite cuddly human, Maximilian Mouse.

I needn't have worried about the weather because next morning the sky was a thin, pale blue across which small patches of cloud were moving from right to left like the electronic patches of rain on a TV weatherman's chart. Kirstie and I kitted ourselves out at the establishment that called itself The Castle Outdoor Shop, and Chas brought out the Land-Rover to drive us down to the quay.

'You got all you want?' he asked me as he got behind the wheel.

'If I remember something later you can fly it out to us,' I said.

'Now hear this!' Chas looked at me over his shoulder. 'No way am I—'

'Oh Chas!' Kirstie said. 'Joke, darling—joke!'

They bickered amiably enough as we rocked downwards and I was reasonably relaxed because we had in fact got all we, or anyone else, could reasonably have wanted. The Outdoor Shop was like a pro's emporium at a well-organized club, running the whole gamut of clubs, bags, sweaters and the rest of the paraphernalia that golfing man is heir to, with the added attraction of a grandiose display of fishing tackle, hill boots, wetsuits and the like. It must have set Chas back a pretty penny to stock but it looked good and, judging from what I'd seen, the customers were satisfyingly impressed. Certainly Kirstie and I had kitted ourselves out without difficulty.

We pulled up where the hotel's inflatable nine-footer was tied up, complete with a 35 h.p. Evinrude to make it go. We unloaded our gear and started stowing it away. As always, I was surprised at how much there was of it. We were already wearing our neoprene wetsuits but by the time we'd got the air bottles into the dinghy, together with harness, regulators, masks, fins and whatever, it looked as though it was going to be a tight fit to get ourselves in as well.

'Now you take good care of him, Kirst,' Chas said. 'Angus here's got to be playing golf tomorrow.' He looked at me. 'You sure you know what you're doing?'

I wondered if he knew what I was doing. 'Just having a look around,' I told him.

'That all?'

I looked up from where I was stowing the gear and caught something about his face I hadn't seen before. Maybe it was no more than the fact that big blond men tend to age all of a sudden when they grow lines around their eyes. Except that Chas's good-natured mug had been lined for years with squinting into a thousand suns over this, that and the other fairway. Even so, the Chas I'd met, first time in years, back at the Walker Galleries, had been his old self, absolutely. Now, unless I was very much mistaken, something was on his mind. Well, no hotelier likes a body on the premises, and it could be that, no more, no less.

I said, 'I'm not on duty, if that's what you mean. Just diving for the hell of it.'

He nodded. 'Take care now, ya hear me?'

I punched the starter button and the outboard snorted itself awake. Up above on the cliff edge the castle cast a long shadow that included the jetty and Chas and the boat and us, and I realized for the first time that it was the front of the castle, with its golf greens and fresh paint, that made the place look like part of the twentieth century. Seeing it even from sea level, it was just what it had always been, a chunk of granite stuck on the edge of a cliff, a left-over from a rougher, tougher age. Have houses got souls? If Chas's

ancestral home did happen to have any thoughts on the
matter, I wondered how it took to its new role. Would a
castle like being a hotel? More to the point, did it enjoy
Chas's attempts at modernization? I studied the rows of
windows looking down on us, the arrowslits and crenellations. All right, so it was whimsy, but the place had a look.
Not a Hammer film look, but a certain something that even
on a clear morning left a quirky feeling of unease. Not that
I should worry, it being no home of mine. But suddenly
unaccountably, I shivered just the same. I turned my back
on the place and steered for open water.

After a while Kirstie said, 'I'm assuming it's the Twins'
wreck you're looking for.'

It was the first time either of us had mentioned the point
of all this, simple bloody-mindedness on my part, but then
I hadn't invited the girl to come along. 'Yes,' I said, 'I want
to have a look at this *Santa Marina*.'

The wind blew hair across her face and she pushed it
away impatiently. 'Do you have to?'

'If you mean am I doing it officially,' I told her, 'the
answer's no.'

'Then why bother?'

'Damn it,' I said, 'because I'm curious. Haven't you had
a look yourself?'

A shake of the head. 'No.'

'Then why now?'

She grinned for the first time. 'Chas thinks one accident
a week's enough, so someone's got to look after you.'

There had been nothing in Chas's manner the previous
night that suggested he'd been keen to detail Kirstie off as
a minder but I let it pass and opened up the map. Local
observation of the Donovans seemed to agree that they
concentrated on a point off the western tip of a pokey little
island called Barrah, some two hundred yards off shore,
apparently at the base of a narrow pinnacle of rock that

stuck up like a tooth from the sea. There was also a frag-
mented ruin of an ancient quay that didn't look the sort of
thing to steer into on a dark night either. I prodded the map
and Kirstie shrugged. So if I wanted to do it, I did it on my
own.

There were worse things to do. I tucked the outboard's
tiller comfortably under my arm and watched the black-
headed gulls bobbing in our wake, like so many plastic toys.
It was a good morning and I felt pleased with my homeland,
wondering why my forebears had ever left it. Probably, I
decided, because they preferred not to starve, but I also
wondered what demon made it so hard for me to leave this
wreck business alone. For all I knew, the books had got it
wrong and the *Santa Marina* sank in these waters after all.
Or it could be a different galleon altogether, which was
highly likely considering the number of Armada vessels
that simply vanished without trace. Why was I worrying,
anyway, when I'd only come up here to play golf?

'How deep is it off Barrah?' Kirstie asked.

'Fifteen metres.' I'd already checked that out on the
charts. Fifteen metres rated as a shallow dive but it was
deep enough in cold water when you haven't been down for
some time.

Kirstie nodded and lay back in the sun with closed eyes.
I wondered what her reaction would have been had I
said, 'Thirty,' and I suspected it would have been much the
same.

It took us the best part of three-quarters of an hour to
reach Barrah, not the most hospitable of shores. Only the
birds seemed to inhabit the two or three square acres that
constituted the island, but it would be possible to manœuvre
a boat between the various outcrops of rock and even tie up
in reasonable safety. I could see how it had been popular
with shark fishers. The sea was astonishingly clear, green-
tinged. Better than I'd expected, I said.

'White sand at the bottom,' Kirstie told me. 'What did you expect—mud?'

I didn't know what I'd expected, so I shut up and got into my harness. I was diving first, so she checked me out, and we made our dive plan.

'What makes you so sure your celestial pair are out of the way?' Kirstie paused with my mask in her hands.

'They're picking up spare engine parts from Mallaig today,' I told her. It was something vouchsafed by the dreaded Basil, only yesterday.

Kirstie made a face at me. 'What's to stop them coming back early, you madman?'

'So they come back early,' I replied. 'They don't own the sea. Anyone can dive in it.'

'All right, all right.' Kirstie put up the diving flag and settled herself on the gunwale. 'Sorry I spoke. Just bring me back a shark.' I snapped my mask once more and rolled over backwards. Splash. Pools of daylight, the dark underside of the boat. What seemed years ago I'd been a golfer, then a policeman. After that I'd taken to writing tales of old-time derring-do and now here I was trying to cope with them all at once. Why does it take us so long to learn our limitations? I waggled my finned feet and drifted down into the translucent world down there, light all of a sudden, free of gravity, a wonder that always came fresh each time.

Diving, you, Straun! Know anything about it?

No, Super. Not a thing.

You going to learn, Straun! Going to learn! You're going to Chatham to let the Navy make a bloody frogman out of you—

Well, there had to be police divers so they could look for missing persons at the bottom of disused canals, abandoned mineworkings and suchlike fun places. I'd done my share too, but not for long, because other things had come up, like a load of shotgun pellets and a permanently short back swing. I slid on down, streaming air bubbles, silver bottles on orange neoprene, a kind of grotesque parody of fish but not ungraceful. Kirstie had been right about the bottom, sand like silver, with the sun catching the stones and slow-moving tendrils of weed around the base of the tooth rock.

The charts had been right, too, the sea bed was exactly fifteen fathoms and I circled, looking about me. Diving off the coast of Britain isn't always fun because currents stir up sand or mud, and visibility can become almost nil, and even in fine weather one swims through a kind of thin soup in which touch is of more practical use than sight. But on this particular day the coast of Scotland was kind, the sort of diving one got off Greece, with the odd unidentified fish appearing now and again to have a look and then scuttling off.

Fish there might be, but no wreck.

For a while I swam rather aimlessly about while I tried to remember what little I'd read on the subject. Obviously I wasn't likely to find myself bumping into the side of a galleon with her gun ports open and the skeletons of Spanish sailors draped around the decks. Not at fifteen metres I wasn't. All that would be left of an Armada wreck would be a barely discernible shape on the sea bottom, perhaps a mere rubble of artefacts left after the wooden hull had rotted away.

After a while I surfaced, hung on to the grab ropes and spat out the mouthpiece of my regulator.

I said, 'Nobody's exactly pinpointed the thing for us. Could be anywhere within half a square mile.'

'So?'

There are plenty of ways for a scuba diver to search methodically for something on the sea bed. Most involve the use of swim lines, all require not just one diver but a team.

I said, 'I'll try again. Then you can have a go.'

Well, there were worse places and it had been a long time since either of us had had a chance to play frogpersons. We dived methodically for most of the morning, turn and turn about, marking out the area we covered by means of stones. It was as businesslike as we could make it, but I was asking myself if it wasn't time we packed it in when the finger of fate intervened during my spell and I found something.

It came looming up directly ahead of me, a dark wall of something that might have been the base of a rock but was not. For a moment I thought absurdly that we'd found the *Santa Marina* and that she really was sitting on the sea bed as though she'd gone down last year. Then I was slapping the hull with the knowledge that if this was her, then Armada galleons had been built with riveted steel plates.

I went up to the surface and waved to Kirstie to bring the boat over to the site before I went down for another look.

I swam around cautiously. Whatever the wreck had been, its remains weren't very impressive, and I guessed it to have been some kind of small trawler. Its deckhouse and superstructure had gone and the hull was rotten with rust; it lay with what remained of its bow nestling cosily at the base of the rock that had caved it in God knows how many years ago.

So it wasn't the *Santa Marina*, but at least it was a return for a morning's diving even if it hardly seemed enough to account for the Donovan brothers' interest. Maybe there was something else? I went up to the side and on to the battered old deck. You could see where the deckhouse had been, and the hatch where presumably the catch had gone, the remains of a winch and some kind of rusted iron housing that I guessed to have been something to do with the trawl. There were some other odds and ends there and I swam over to have a closer look because there was something familiar about them. A couple of iron pulleys? Like hell they were. I picked one of them up.

It was a cannon ball.

*

I looked at that ball for some time, because even in the refracted light of the water it said something to me. One cannon ball looks very like another, but this was one in a million because, as I turned it over, the clear, kite-shaped scar on the surface that I'd noticed back at Sid Walker's gallery stood out bright and clear. It didn't just look like the same one, it *was* the same one. The very ball that Mr Smith of Islington had nicked was the one I was holding in my hand.

I put the thing down and moved along the deck to see what else there might be waiting for someone to discover. The bow area was just a mass of shadow where weed from the rocks had grown over it, but trailing over the side was a newish rope so I followed it down. It was pretty dark down there too, but I could see the outline of the hole the rock had gashed in the plating in some storm long ago. Maybe no storm, but fog. Or the skipper was drunk. I pushed weed aside and flashed my torch around but there didn't seem a lot to see so I turned round to come out of the shadows of that gently waving forest and then stopped.

One of the twins was blocking the way and the harpoon gun he was holding was pointing roughly in the direction of my heart.

We stood and looked at each other. With the light from the surface I could see well enough that it was Sean because of the tattoo on the back of his hand; the rest of him was covered by a black wet suit.

I kept very still. At that moment I didn't know whether he could see me or not but nobody likes to have a harpoon gun trained on his middle and I didn't want Sean Donovan to mistake me for a desirable fish. Then he moved his face a fraction and the eyes behind his mask met mine.

It was a moment of truth all right, because something telepathic passed between us and all at once I was back at that bank and that shotgun was lined up on me and the raider's eyes were staring into mine through the opening of his Balaclava helmet. I'd known in that moment that he intended to kill me, and now, as I looked through the mask glass and met Sean Donovan's pale eyes, I got the same message loud and clear. He knew I was no fish but he was going to shoot me just the same. I watched mesmerized as the tip of the harpoon shifted slightly while the young maniac adjusted his aim. On land I might have tried to jump him but fifty feet down you simply can't move fast enough. Then somewhere above me, at the extreme limits of my peripheral vision, something moved.

It can be extremely difficult to overcome an instinctive movement, particularly when self-preservation is involved. I knew that if I looked up at that moment, Sean would do the same, but I was uncomfortably certain that it was brother Patrick up there, doubtless armed with another gun. So I looked up, and so did Sean, but by then it was too late for him to do anything about what happened next. The person above wasn't Patrick, it was Kirstie; Kirstie cradling in her hands the cannon ball I'd left up there. I watched fascinated as, with a rather graceful gesture, she opened her hands and dropped her iron sphere in the rough direction of Sean Donovan's head.

I very nearly felt sorry for Sean. It must have been one hell of a moment, to stare up and find something like that coming down on top of him. Whether he really managed to avoid the eight pounds or so of pig iron by jerking his head back at the right moment, or whether Kirstie's aim was bad, I never found out. Probably the latter, because the refraction of light in water makes it notoriously difficult to know exactly where things are. Be that as it may, her missile skated down the front of his wet suit and landed on his left foot.

Christ! I thought, and felt my teeth clamp over my air pipe in sympathetic agony, though not so much sympathy that I didn't find time to grab the harpoon gun. By rights a cannon ball dropped from that height should have turned a human foot into a slushy mess. It certainly didn't do it any good, but the combination of his ribbed flipper and the shifting sand beneath it saved him from the worst.

But he needed a helping hand to reach the surface just the same.

CHAPTER 9

He'd swum out from Barrah, so we took him back there where Patrick was waiting. Once on the beach you could see their Sea Chief tied up behind an outcrop of rock, the damn thing had been invisible from the sea.

'You're after breaking my foot,' Sean said. He sat on the beach with his mask and flippers off and, while his face was white under its tan, his foot was every colour you could think of. Patrick, in sweater and jeans, patted it gently dry with a towel before looking up at us with a cold hatred that was startling. He said, 'And isn't there a law against doing such things.'

'There's a law about trying to shoot people with a harpoon gun, too,' I said. 'And don't tell me about the law or I'll have the local police spend a day or two making you prove how legal you are. The Excise men, too.'

'And what is it we're smuggling?' Sean asked sulkily, apparently not liking talk of Excise men, who are good chaps but thorough. 'You should not have been diving where you were.'

'So you're the registered owners of that old sardine can?'

I asked. And when he didn't answer, 'Now tell me about the harpoon gun.'

'I use it for small shark,' Sean said. 'That's what I thought you were. With all those shadows down there it's easy to make mistakes, so it is.'

I'd been the one at the sharp end of that gun and Sean had known well enough I was no shark, but as a story it would just about hold up, because if Sean had dived from the Sea Chief, he wouldn't necessarily have seen the hotel's boat. In which case it was possible—just marginally possible—that he hadn't known I was there. Hadn't Chas himself stated that shark was still hunted on and off in these waters? *A tragic mistake, m'lud, and my client bitterly regrets—*

'It's a darlin' man you are,' I said. 'So why don't you just tell me what it is you two are up to?'

Two pairs of pale eyes regarded me with absolutely no expression. Finally Patrick said, 'It's nothing at all we're up to. Diving's not against the law.'

'It's not against the law to buy bits of maritime antiquery, either,' I agreed, 'but I'm curious to know why you drop them back in the sea just so that you can say they came from a non-existent Armada wreck.'

Sean was flexing his foot cautiously, a poor thing to look at but apparently nothing broken. He said, 'It's a crime?'

'It would be if you tried to sell them,' I told him. Though I wasn't entirely sure, because a genuine sixteenth-century cannon ball is still a genuine cannon ball the second time around. Oh well.

'We're not selling them, man!'

'Then why do it?'

They thought about that one. Finally Patrick said, 'Well now, it's by way of being a joke. This friend of ours is swearing that there's no wreck in these waters, an' we're swearing that there is. He's an old fellow who can't go diving for himself so we thought we'd be having a bit of fun with him dropping a few bits and pieces down and then having them photographed as they're brought up.'

His eyes didn't seem to be part of the fun. His eyes said he was sorry his brother hadn't killed me.

'Well, a sense of humour helps the world go round,' I said. 'I hope the Donovans manage to keep smiling in gaol, where I'm sure you'll end up.'

Sean's body twitched, his foot must have been hurting like the devil. He said softly, 'There's a—'

'Yes?'

He shook his head. 'Nothing. Go back home, Inspector. There's nothin' for you here, and you know it.'

I did indeed know it and the knowledge didn't please me. On the way home in the inflatable I brooded on the frustrations of living in a society where it's not done for the police force to work citizens over with a length of rubber hose. I also wondered what clever ploy I'd have thought up if Kirstie hadn't turned up with her cannon ball act.

'How the devil did you know he was there?' I asked her eventually.

'I spotted his air trail.' Kirstie didn't sound smug, which did her credit. 'He swam almost underneath me and I could see he'd got a harpoon gun at the ready, so I thought you'd better know. It didn't seem a good idea to hang about.'

She most certainly hadn't hung about, because with no time to put her gear on, she'd had to hold her breath for the whole fifteen metres down and back again, to say nothing of the weight-putting exercise in between. 'You'd have looked silly if he hadn't been meaning to spear me,' I said.

Kirstie grinned. 'Not half so silly as you'd have looked if I'd let him.'

True. All the same, I wondered just how she'd been so sure. A wetsuit is reasonably warm in water but it's a poor thing to wear in a windy boat. Kirstie had left her anorak behind and refused to take mine, so in the end we shared it. To start with, I found myself remembering the last words I'd had with Patrick.

'*I hope the Donovans manage to keep smiling in gaol—*'

And Sean had said, '*There's a—*'

And stopped. What had he been going to say? *There's a Donovan there already and he's still smiling*?

After a while Kirstie shivered and moved closer to me and I began to think about something else.

All the same, I made a couple of phone calls before I went to bed. There were probably a lot of Donovans behind bars in Ulster but the RUC were proud of their big computer and it seemed a pity it shouldn't have its chance.

I always used to wake early when I'd a match and I seemed not to have lost the trick of it, because the next morning saw me out of bed before the alarm had a chance to ring. I peered down at that by now familiar bit of golf course below. Still there. The first tee and a fairway, the ninth green with a flag flapping on the end of a pole, and, thanks be to God, a clear sky. I moved my shoulders experimentally and, though they were sore, that was all. Well, at least you knew where you were with golf, I thought, because for all its endless permutations, it boiled down to getting a small ball into a slightly larger hole. People's behaviour in the world beyond the greens was a lot less predictable, nevertheless today I was not a policeman. I was playing in a Pro-Celebrity golf match because I was what the public chose to call a well-known author.

I switched on the television in search of the weather. The thing seemed to have partially cured itself because I got a forecast, though with a lot of interference. Fine, the man was saying, through a snowstorm. West coast of Scotland would be dry and fine.

The phone rang. It was Chas. 'You there, boy? You

feeling good?' The prospect of a game seemed to have done wonders for everyone this morning.

I made noises like I was feeling great.

'Then get on down here and play some golf!'

I got on down.

Every competition has its own atmosphere, in my experience those for amateurs being tenser, bitchier and generally less fun than those on the professional circuit where the same chaps slog it out more or less amicably for three-quarters of the year. The big Pro-Celebrity games fall somewhere between the two, both sides being highly professional in their own way and neither too worried about the game. Why should they be? The golfer isn't risking his place in the prize money ratings and the celebrity is only a weekend player anyway. Both are indulging in a little show business and, with nothing to lose, there is no reason why everyone shouldn't have a good time, sponsors included.

On this particular morning, the atmosphere was, if anything, better than usual, probably because Chas MacLiven's organization was pretty free and easy. So far as I knew, nobody was actually being paid. There was no television coverage and indeed no publicity of any kind, the whole thing being a private lark for the guests at the hotel. Consequently the general milling around had much of the cheerful chaos of a club competition except that at no club of which I'd been a member had so much hard liquor circulated immediately after breakfast.

'Hi, Angus! You having a dram before you go out?' Chas shouldering his way out of the bar, as big as a moose in golf gear, if you call tartan trews that, and a glass of something whisky-coloured in his hand.

I chickened out of the drink, too early for me and whatever other excuse came to hand. I knew not why, everyone else seemed to be knocking it back and showing every intention of carrying on. Luther Koch, the pro playing Gabriel Banda, waved a beer at me from the far side of the room, where he was drinking with the big black cricketer. Most of the non-playing hotel guests were hard at it too, and I even glimpsed Mr Meuse, resplendent in a kind of blue battle-dress, a drink in one hand and a camera case in the other, deep in chat with an elderly character who was talking finance. Everybody, but everybody, was determined to have a wonderful time.

Kirstie pushed her way through the log jam of people, carrying in her arms a startled-looking Cairn terrier, and waggled the animal at me. 'Mrs Bewley's,' she said. 'We've been walkies.' She was wearing blue linen slacks and a heavy cream Aran knit jacket with a shawl collar. It was right for her and right for the day and it reflected nothing whatever of Chas's Rob Roy outfit.

'Very nice,' I told her.

'You should have come too.'

I looked at her. I thought I saw in her eyes something that might have been an appeal. I don't know what she found in mine. She said, 'Straun—'

'Now listen, FOLKS!' Chas standing on a chair, shouting to make himself heard above the din. 'Listen, y'all! Get yourselves a drink and come on out because we're sure as hell going to play some GOLF!'

My God, I thought, and this was the man the critics used to say was *dull*. Chas on the circuit had never touched anything stronger than coffee, but different days different manners. All the same, if this was 9.30 in the morning, it had all the makings of a roughish day. We went outside into the early autumn sunshine, blue sky but with a haze out to sea. I sniffed the air, remembering.

I said, 'We shan't have to hang about—there'll be a sea mist later on.'

'Weather centre or old Scottish know-how?'

'Neither. But it's warmish here and there's a cool breeze

coming in from the Atlantic. Put the two together, you get fog.' I was reasonably certain of my facts, but not unduly worried about weather. I asked, 'Have you seen my clubs? Chas was laying on a caddie for me.'

'I told him to unlay,' Kirstie said. 'I'll caddie.'

'Caddie for Chas, then.'

'It was his idea. Besides, he wouldn't want me. He's got a lad who always caddies for him.'

Golf-wise it mattered not at all. With a real course and a real match, a local caddie meant two or three strokes a round, but for this kind of lark it was probably neither here nor there. I wished it was only a matter of golf. So many decisions, so often the wrong ones.

'I've a full set of clubs in the bag,' I warned her. 'It'll be heavy.'

'Oh Straun, don't be absurd. I'll use a trolley.'

Well, why shouldn't a caddie use a trolley? Because they didn't, that was why, but this was hardly serious golf. I looked round. The guests were beginning to spread them-selves around the first tee and down alongside the fairway. There were a couple of small figures in full Highland dress and for a moment I had a genuine sense of foreboding in case Chas had organized cheer leaders. A few twirling Scottish batons was about all the morning needed, but it turned out that they were miniature pipers instead. We had a few fairly brave skirls. Luther Koch and Gabriel Banda came over trailing real Scots caddies and we chatted amiably until the bagpipes faded away into small wails and Chas took over on the microphone. He said what a great event this was going to be, how special it was to the MacLiven Hotel. It could have sounded ridiculous but in fact he did it very well. What unrecorded ancestor had bequeathed Chas MacLiven the gift of the gab I found it hard to imagine, because it was unlikely to have been any of the lairds who'd ruled the castle on Sarne. Perhaps some black sheep

MacLiven had strayed into a more vocal pasture, happenings about which I very much doubted if Chas knew himself.

'Now I don't have to introduce the three guests we have playing today, do I, folks?'

Well, maybe he didn't have to, but of course he did, looking for all the world like a bad painting of a laird rallying the clans. The words fairly rolled out. 'A big welcome for that legendary batsman, Gabriel Banda.' 'And a hand for Britain's latest best-selling author.' Plus, for Luther Koch, '. . . the new golf star from West Germany.' The first game would be Koch and Banda against himself and Angus Straun. The winners to get this and that. Luther first off.

'*Mein Gott*,' Luther said under his breath, 'in my country we haf ways of stopping you talking.'

'Just hit that ball,' I said, 'or we'll be here all day.'

Luther nodded, waved his clubhead vaguely in the air behind his teed-up ball and then swung. The club dropped quite some way below the horizontal, then slashed back like a flail. Nobody had ever accused Luther of being a poem of motion but he could knock a ball prodigious distances, quite often in the right direction. I watched this particular one climb into the sky, flying straight down the middle for a long one. There was a scatter of applause.

In Pro-Celebrity games both professionals play first and I watched Chas drive with interest. How much he'd drunk since breakfast I'd no idea, but it seemed likely to have at least some bearing on the day's play.

'Man,' he said to no one in particular, 'I just love this game.' Unlike Luther, he had a swing to wonder at. A lovely, slow, easy thing I'd forgotten how good it was to watch. Big men are often light on their feet. Chas gave the impression of being light all over, so unhurried you could watch his weight move from right to left, the right wrist coming over, the high, classic follow through that looked like a diagram from a how-to-do-it text book.

Smack. The ball as straight as Luther's but further and to more applause. Now for the little boy's turn. I pushed in a peg and balanced the ball on it, remembering a one-time hang-up about the first ball of the day. It was a thing that could spook you if you let it, and I'd got over it during my first season of serious competition. All at once, for the first time in years, that same feeling again.

I made my mind a blank, drove safely enough, somewhere to the right of the fairway, perhaps in short rough but nothing to worry about, and waited while Gabriel did the same.

He said, 'My word, it is a long way.' Which was true because the first must have been nearly five hundred yards, which is a long way for a nine-hole course and longer still when you're playing on an island with the built-in feeling that you can go off the edge at any time. But he didn't have to worry, because like most good cricketers he had the rhythm that makes a golfer, and his drive was accurate enough though shorter than I'd expected. Nevertheless, in spite of the general chaos, we were off and all that lay before us was a day's golf.

Pro-Am golf is played on the Stableford scoring system, which means that the four players concerned play for points rather than for strokes or simply the hole. Handicaps are taken into account, and players are awarded a point for a bogey of one under par, two for level par and three for a birdie—an arrangement that ensures that the weaker players still play a significant part in the game.

I did well enough on the opening hole because, being a long one, I received a stroke and had no great difficulty in making my two points, unfair to Luther who only made the same when he chipped in brilliantly to get down in a stroke less. Out of the corner of my eye I'd checked that Gabriel Banda had only managed a bogey where Chas dropped in an extraordinary putt from the edge of the green for a birdie, which made their overall score for the hole the same.

There are few things duller than a blow-by-blow account of a golf match, unless it's to an audience who knows the course in question and knows to an inch exactly how hard or simple it is to produce a given figure for any particular hole. Our first round of nine holes took an hour and a half, leaving the score all square, and speaking for myself, I enjoyed it very much. Considering that I hadn't played at all for nigh on a couple of months, I wasn't doing all that badly. Nor for that matter was my caddie, who pulled with a will and kept her mouth shut. All in all, I was beginning to enjoy myself.

Chas crossed the green in my direction, looking more moose-like than ever and slightly bright-eyed, even though he'd been playing some remarkable golf. 'Right, fellers, a short break before the second nine. Get a couple of quick ones in.'

Well, a small one wouldn't do any harm. Banda was beaming expansively, spinning a putter in his hand. He really was a big chap who looked as though he'd hit a ball a mile, which on a good day he very nearly could.

We had our pause for refreshment, Luther shrugging his shoulders and diving in with the rest. The spectators, who weren't having to bother about hitting balls anyway, gave every sign of becoming totally pi-eyed.

'This is a hell of a way to run a golf match,' I said to Kirstie. 'And go easy on that stuff, I don't want you towing my gear the wrong way.'

'You look after your liquor, Straun, and I'll look after mine.'

I wondered vaguely where her Mr Mouse had got to but there was no sign of him. If he'd been drinking along with the rest of the crew, my guess was he'd already hibernated for the winter. I shivered suddenly as a chill wind stirred the flags, and Kirstie noticed.

'Sweater?' Golf may not have been her game but the girl was a born caddie.

I said, 'May as well,' and as I got one out of the pocket of my bag I saw Banda do the same, which was understandable, northern weather not being his thing. Then Chas was making encouraging noises over a hand-held loudhailer, glasses were put down and we were off again.

The second nine was a good bit wilder than the first, which wasn't all that surprising. Nobody was going to wrap a club round a tree or make a complete nonsense of a hole but they were going to take the odd chance, with the result that there were one or two remarkable birdies and several pretty disastrous two under pars. As we came up to the sixth, I think Chas and I were a couple of points ahead, which was what encouraged Luther to try his hand at something he'd have left alone had he been stone cold sober.

'Time we had a go,' he said at the tee.

I guessed what was in his mind, and rather him than me. The sixth ran along the western side of the island for about a hundred and fifty yards and then dog-legged inland round a massive outcrop of granite. From what I'd been told, the accepted way to play the hole was to slam one right down the middle with just enough draw to carry it round the corner. A hook and you were over the cliff, a slice and you could bounce anywhere off the granite. The alternative for the brave or plain foolhardy was to cut the corner by going over the top of the obstacle—easy enough from close to with a lofted club but more of a problem from way back on the tee. A short iron wouldn't make the distance and something longer would be pushed for height.

From the far side of the fairway, I could see Luther squinting up at the rock, suddenly not as clear as it had been. I glanced out to sea where the horizon had vanished completely and there was a mist coming up.

'Six iron, Jock.'

The caddie fished out the club, looking doubtful. With an uncertain wind blowing, things were getting less easy and we were going to look pretty daft if the ball landed on top of the granite and stayed there.

Luther teed up and drove with everything he had, club face open to get the ball high . . . and hooked it wildly to the left, straight for the cliff.

He said something rude in German, tossed the club to his caddie and waited, fuming, while Chas made his shot, straight to the turn where he wanted to be. Banda and I played a couple of safe ones and we all moved off after our balls.

Which was the moment when the fog came down.

Sea fogs are different from the kind one gets on the mainland, they are colder, swifter and less predictable. This was a fair-sized patch, a white, dank cloud rolling in over the top of the cliff like the carbon dioxide they use for the witches' scene in *Macbeth*. Luther and Gabriel had been totally swallowed up in it and I wondered how near the cliff edge the German had been before that billowing mass had hit him.

'Hell of a time to come down,' Chas was saying behind me. 'Another half-hour and we'd have been back.' He tramped towards where the others had vanished and he himself disappeared.

Kirstie and I stood there on our own and listened in the sudden rather oppressive quiet. The gulls had stopped their crying and, apart from the sea, all other small incidental sounds seemed to have been deadened by the murk.

'Luther!' I shouted and listened, and this time we got a reply. For a moment I thought it was a gull, but no gull sounded quite like that. It was a long high cry of human terror that shrieked to its immediate crescendo, then receded, falling, falling until it was gone.

CHAPTER 10

Chief Superintendent George Neale was a small, neat man with the kind of raw-boned, high-coloured face that seems to go with a life in the open air and cold climates. Out of uniform he'd have made a very passable ghillie; dressed for work in the Chief's room at Mallardoch police station he was impressive, with the built-in aggression that seems part and parcel of men built like terriers.

He said, 'You're not on duty, Inspector.'

'No, sir.' He wasn't asking a question because he knew the answer already, he was simply reminding me. I added in order to remind him, 'I'm simply a guest of Mr MacLiven's, staying at his hotel.'

'At which two other guests have died within a few days of each other.'

'Yes.'

'Are you suggesting the deaths were no accidental?' He would have made a good radio interviewer, socking it to 'em regardless.

I said, 'No, sir. No such suggestion at all. I just thought I'd ask if anything similar has happened in the area recently.'

'If there's some kind of pattern, you're meaning?'

I said, 'Well, sir, yes.'

The Chief Superintendent's chilly blue eyes bored into mine. If he had really been a terrier his whiskers would have been quivering. Then unexpectedly he smiled. 'Man, there are always accidents up here. Some fool or other falling off Ben Nevis or drowning himself in a loch. I'll grant you that they don't often break their necks falling into dungeons but the inquest this morning on the man Werner recorded accidental death, which so far as I'm concerned is very sensible. Now we've got this golfing laddie of yours who walks off a cliff in the middle of a thick fog.' He began rearranging the pencils on his desk so as to make a neat square. 'Damn it, Straun, you were *there*! From what I hear, the wee man was drunk as a lord.'

News got around, I thought. Oh well. I said, 'Luther Koch certainly wasn't drunk.'

But ye'll not deny that there'd been a drop or three taken over breakfast?'

'There was a drop or four taken by some people,' I agreed, 'but I doubt if Koch—'

'You doubt but you don't know.'

I shrugged. 'I wasn't watching him that closely. He'd had a few beers, yes, but he was playing too good golf to be drunk.'

'I'm knowing a man who can *only* play when he's drink taken.' Neale began making a rectangle out of his pencil square. 'What's worrying you, Straun, is that Werner and Koch were both German.'

'Koch was German,' I said. 'Werner happened to be an Afrikaaner but certainly they were both foreigners.'

'And that worries you?'

'It's an odd coincidence.' There were far odder coincidences every day, but how does one describe that purely personal sense of unease we call a hunch?

Neale rubbed his chin, apparently reading my mind. 'Are you just having a bad feeling about this or is there something more?'

There was a little matter of being pushed off a train, and the distinctly odd behaviour of the Heavenly Twins, but just how much hard fact did it amount to?

'No,' I said. 'I've got nothing more.'

Neale jumbled his pencils all up again and put them back in their jam pot. 'Then I suggest you go back to your friend MacLiven and go on playing golf. Unless the inquest on Koch comes up with something other than accidental death —which it certainly won't—there's nothing to investigate.' He stood up and we shook hands. 'A pleasure to meet you, Inspector. Tell MacLiven not to be so free with his drink in future.'

I was half way through the door before he remembered that he was holding a Telex for me from Belfast. I put it in my pocket and went on down the road to the library, where I read the answer to my telephoned inquiry of the day before. According to the computer, Crumlin Road at present housed one Terence Donovan, aged fifty-two, who was serving a twelve-year sentence on account of his involvement in the bombing of a public house in 1987. He had twin sons, Sean and Patrick, aged twenty-six. Neither had so far been convicted of anything. Both were known and active members of the IRA.

I sat there on one of the library's stackable fibreglass chairs and tried to work out a link between Irish terrorists, non-existent Armada wrecks and accident-prone visitors. After a while I gave up because I hadn't much time, as I was due to meet Chas in half an hour and we were going back to the island together. I put the Telex back in my pocket and started working my way through the library's Large Volume section of 934.24 (Photography) instead.

It is a mistake to assume that a couple of fatal accidents cast a sense of doom over a hotel. It depresses the management because good hoteliers feel responsible for the wellbeing of their patrons and dread the resultant paperwork when things go wrong. Guests, on the other hand, seem to take a ghoulish delight in having something to talk about and give a distinct impression that there's nothing like something nasty happening to someone else to lighten up the day. But Chas and Kirstie were distinctly management and back at the castle that evening I felt the weight they were carrying. Chas in particular. If you insist on being a musical comedy Scotsman, you have to have a certain lightness of touch to carry it off, whereas Chas seemed to be getting dangerously close to playing the classic role of the clown with a breaking heart.

'Come up and have a drink at my place,' he had said after dinner. 'My place' was the suite of rooms he kept on the first floor, not furnished in Highland primitive but colonial American, most underrated of periods. Kirstie was there, in a sweater and tweed skirt, a single row of pearls round her neck. There was a real fire in the grate and the flames warmed her natural pallor and picked deep lights from her hair. Then the phone went and Chas answered it.

'I got to go down to the bar a minute. Give him a drink, Kirst.'

He went and she gave me a drink. I said, 'Chas seems to be taking all this a bit hard.'

'Yes.' She fixed one for herself, talking to me over her shoulder. 'He's put in a lot of work on this place.'

I nodded. 'He certainly seems to have gone overboard on the Scottish bit.'

Kirstie smiled. She had a slow, reflective smile, not like Laurie's whiplash reaction to amusement. Kirstie was Highlands, Laurie pure urban. Would each have been like the other if their backgrounds had been reversed? Kirstie, Highland Kirstie, said, 'Americans are great people for enthusiasm, great people for their roots, too. I know Chas looks comic but it's real, you know. He loves this place and the people. It hurts him that they don't like him back.'

'Don't they?' But I'd noticed the withdrawn looks of those women by their cottages. I said, 'Scots don't accept new things but he's the MacLiven, after all.'

'No, he's not.' Kirstie kicked a glowing coal. 'He's an honorary MacLiven.'

I'd forgotten that. 'They'll get used to him,' I told her. 'Is that all that he's got on his mind?'

'Isn't that enough?'

'I suppose so.'

Kirstie reached out for my glass and our hands touched and hastily untouched. As she went to the drinks table she looked over her shoulder. 'Fair's fair, Straun. Now tell me what you've got on your mind.'

I took my drink. I could have turned the question easily enough but fair's fair, the girl had saved my life. I said, 'You know what it's like when you find yourself in a roomful of people who are wildly dissimilar but obviously know each other terribly well? You try to discover why. *Why* is that obviously shifty character such a friend of the parson? What *is* it that the boy from a West End chorus line has in common with that cosy soul who's plainly a suburban housewife? Puzzle: find the thread that ties them all together.'

Kirstie said, 'It wouldn't worry me at all but I can see it does you. So?'

'So somebody tried to kill me on the train coming up here. A couple of IRA hit men are pretending to be hippies and looking for a wreck that doesn't exist. We've got a photographer who takes pictures of the wrong things and what strike me as two extremely dubious accidental deaths.' I swallowed what I'd taken to be well-watered Scotch and discovered it to be straight, pale-coloured malt. I said huskily, 'There's a thread that links all that somewhere, but I'm damned if I know what it is.'

'Oh, Straun!' Kirstie said softly. 'It's not your problem. I keep saying it, but really why don't you just go home?'

'Why don't we all go home?' And when I saw the hurt in her eyes: 'I'm sorry.'

'Forget it,' Kirstie said. Only, of course, when a woman says, 'Forget it,' forgetting is the last thing she intends to do.

I put my glass down. 'Thanks for the drink, anyway. When Chas comes back, tell him I've gone up to change.'

She didn't look at me, so I walked out and shut the door behind me.

I was getting used to my room. At first it had been a joke, with its vast four-poster and the gilt fittings in the bathroom. Now I felt vaguely ill at ease in it. No reason, save the far-fetched idea that the castle didn't particularly like being tarted up, which was tweely fanciful, not my thing at all. I took my shoes off and looked at the pictures, uninspired but pleasant enough litho prints of fur and forest with the odd seascape thrown in which I guessed had been supplied as per contract by whoever had masterminded the room. There was an abstract that struck me as being the odd man out, disturbingly humanoid and female but unintelligible to me, no expert in these things.

Which was the moment I became aware that there was someone in the room next door.

It took me a moment to register the fact that this was out of the ordinary, neighbours being common in hotels, then another to remember that the room next door had been meant for Laurie, Chas's tactful handling of a relationship he hadn't been sure about.

I switched out the light and went over to the door, quiet enough in my socks. There was always the chance that, finding me on my own, Chas had let the room, but unlikely without checking first. Equally unlikely a guest would be getting settled in the dark, since there was no light showing beneath the door. I listened and it seemed quiet enough, but once you've got wind of someone, even a tomb sounds as though a regiment's marching through it, so I stood and listened until the sound I couldn't hear came roughly level with the door and then I smacked it open as hard as I could. Somebody gave a grunt as the door hit him and then I was through and turning, grabbing at whatever came first, which happened to be an arm.

In the murk of the unlit room I heard a gasp of pain, but I lugged my catch to the wall and used my free hand to switch on the light.

'You're hurting me.' Kirstie's favourite furry man. Mr Mouse.

'I'll hurt you a damn sight more if you don't tell me what you're up to,' is what I nearly told him, but policemen are not supposed to say that kind of thing and I was already feeling guilty enough. Poor Mr Mouse. Kirstie would never forgive me.

In the end I said, 'Mr Meuse, suppose you tell me exactly what you're doing here.'

A blink behind the big glasses. 'The wrong room, I think.'

Seen close to, he didn't really look like a mouse. In fact, he had the kind of round, all-purpose face that seems to be the special preserve of central European stock, a kind of clothes horse on which to hang the personality of their choice. Mr Mouse's was fronted by a pair of dark brown eyes that regarded me with a kind of quiet reproach. I've done nothing to you, they said, so why are you proposing something unpleasant for me?

I sighed. 'Look,' I began reasonably, 'you can't really expect me to believe you came into this room by mistake.'

He said mildly, 'I don't see why not. My room is directly below this. I got the floor wrong, that's all.'

'What about the key?'

'The door wasn't locked.'

My God, I thought, he can't really expect me to believe that. But then, why not? It might be true. Might. 'Mr Meuse,' I said, 'forget about the room. Just tell me what you're really doing on this island.'

'I'm on vacation.' He paused as though feeling he should add something to that. 'Kind of looking around and taking some pictures.'

'What of?'

Mr Meuse smiled. 'You're a policeman, Mr Straun. There's no law that says I can't photograph the Scottish highlands.'

'On 35 millimetre with a stack of long lenses?'

This time he raised his eyebrows. 'But there *is* a law about the equipment you use?'

'No,' I agreed, 'but things get a bit tighter when it comes to names. As a matter of interest, is your name really Meuse?'

'Yes, really Meuse. You want to see my passport?'

'I'd be interested.'

He nodded. 'OK, then. You better come down to my room.'

I went. He really did have the room below.

'Feel free, Mr Straun.' He fished in the drawer of the bedside table and held out his passport. It was Israeli, with Mr Mouse's sad face looking out at me from Page 2. Maximilian Meuse, Company Director, born Kever, Hungary, 1921. Height five feet seven inches, weight one hundred and thirty pounds, eyes brown, hair grey, no distinguishing features. Religion Jewish.

I handed it back. 'Looks kosher, Mr Meuse.'

'I assure you it is kosher, Mr Straun.'

'Then suppose,' I said, 'we quit the comedy duo bit and get down to business, such as the fact that the television sets in this hotel all make use of a common aerial. They happen to be tapped into that aerial just outside the window of that room upstairs, and you went there this evening to make a repair.'

If Maximilian Meuse blinked, I didn't see it. 'Now why should I do that?'

It was the kind of question that he might reasonably have supposed I'd have countered with 'Suppose you tell me.' But fortunately he didn't have to tell me because I knew the answer already. 'Because,' I told him, 'you didn't make a very good job of it the first time.'

Did those brown eyes look marginally more soulful? They should have done, but it was hard to tell. But he did make a rather Jewish gesture of dismissal. It said more readily than words that I was wasting his time. Well all right, Mr Mouse, go down fighting by all means.

I said, 'You disconnected the main TV aerial yesterday so that nobody would be tempted to see a programme on BBC2 called "For Your Bookshelf", which was being broadcast at nine o'clock. You also got rid of the newspapers that carried the day's programmes. You reconnected the aerial later but not very well, so you came back to make a better job of it. Now why should you do all that, Mr Meuse?'

His shoulders moved fractionally. It was not a shrug, more a fatalistic tremor. 'Why indeed, Mr Straun?'

'Because you were on the box, that's why. Just for the record,' I asked, 'which *are* you—Meuse or Abraham?'

'Meuse.' He sat down slowly and motioned to me to do the same. 'Abraham's just the name I work under. How did you know?'

'This is a great area for photographers,' I told him. 'The local public library has got three of your books for a start. I found them very interesting.'

Mr Mouse asked drily, 'You are an ornithologist?'

'I'm afraid I only read the introductions and the publishers' blurbs,' I confessed, 'but they put me on the right track to find out a bit more about you. You're not only a world-famous bird photographer but you're a member of the Wiesenthal as well.'

The Wiesenthal Foundation is a private Vienna-based organization for tracking down such surviving war criminals

as are still at large. It was a Wiesenthal operation that had
Eichmann snatched from his hideout in Brazil in 1972, and
a single Foundation member who had kidnapped Herman
Sachs in New York a year later. By all accounts, they were
as tough a group of activists as one would be likely to find
anywhere. Mr Mouse didn't look like an Israeli hit man,
but then, who did?

We looked at each other. My move. Your move. You did,
I didn't. The old challenges left over from schooldays,
which when you get down to basics just seem to prove how
remarkably little we learn. I think that perhaps the same
thought occurred to Meuse, because I saw him smile slightly
before he said, 'The Wiesenthal Foundation is not a pro-
scribed organization.'

'It's not,' I agreed, 'but some of its activities are. If you
try to abduct some ex-concentration camp commandant
from the UK, you're liable to cause a certain amount
of fuss. You're not allowed to knock off war criminals
either.'

'That hardly makes the United Kingdom unique.' Meuse
frowned at me suddenly in a slightly old-maidish way.
'Come, Mr Straun, I do not deny that I have a certain
sympathy with the organization you mention. I may even
have been associated with it from time to time, but you can
hardly imagine that I am here to kidnap someone and carry
him off to Israel. For one thing, my work has been largely
concerned with long-range photographic identification.
Also, although I admit my father died in Dachau, I myself
am somewhat over combatant age.'

'I know,' I said, 'I wasn't necessarily thinking of abduc-
tion.'

'Then what—' Meuse's already expressive eyes opened
suddenly wide as he caught on. 'Mr Straun, you are surely
not suggesting that I had anything to do with the death of
that unfortunate young man yesterday? Even if the Wiesen-

thal was a crude execution squad, which it certainly is not, Luther Koch was not even born during the holocaust.'

'I know,' I said, 'but suppose you tell me exactly where you were when Koch went over that cliff.' All I needed was a notebook and a blunt pencil to be the classic stage copper, but if you gotta ask, you gotta ask.

Some kind of gull hurtled past the window with a scream and Meuse glanced towards it with instinctive interest. Had I been pointing a gun at him, I imagine his reaction would have been much the same. The cry of the bird died away and Meuse said, 'I was walking by myself, with a book and a camera. I wasn't with anyone. I ask you, Mr Straun, what do I know about golf?'

'I'm afraid,' I said, 'that walking by yourself isn't much of an alibi.' But I suspected that if I asked the same question of half the people in the hotel I'd have got much the same answer. Come to that, when Luther had vanished into the mist, Chas had been hidden, too. Where had he and Gabriel Banda been in the white-out, or Ailsa McCrae for that matter? It's the sensible villains who make sure of their alibis, the good guys never know they should have one.

'Look,' I said, 'I agree there seems no reason to suppose *anyone* killed Koch. On the other hand, you must admit your behaviour has been less than frank.' The slightly pained approach seemed appropriate and I rather liked 'less than frank'.

Meuse nodded.

'So why don't you tell me exactly what it is you're doing here?'

He thought it over. Finally he said, 'If I tell you, can you keep it between the two of us?'

'I can't answer that because I don't know what you're going to tell me.' It was a daft thing to ask, as he must have known.

Mr Mouse made one of his defeated gestures. 'It is

probably nothing. *Nothing*, you understand? With war criminals there are always rumours, usually fantastic. But then
the whole thing is fantastic, so where does one stop?' He
looked at me as though he expected me to tell him. I didn't,
and he went on. 'Some time ago we picked up a man called
Roschmann. Not wanted himself directly but in trouble
about something else. When questioned, he produced a story
which he offered as a piece of negotiation.'

'Yes,' I said, 'go on.'

'This Roschmann had been an ordinary seaman in the
German Navy, the Kriegsmarine, during the war. Nobody
important, not responsible for anything, you understand.
But he thought we would be interested in the last operation
in which he took part. It seems he was a member of the
crew of some kind of high-speed motorboat—a motor torpedo boat, I think, and late in 1943 he accompanied his
boat to the west coast of Scotland. The mission was highly
secret and was subject to extraordinary security because the
trip was not part of normal naval operations. Roschmann
should have known nothing but he was a member of the
crew, and it must be hard to keep secrets on a little boat.
Roschmann said that by then even ordinary sailors knew
the war was lost and that important men were already
getting their money out of Germany. That was the job they
and their torpedo boat were going to do.'

'And which particular rat was leaving the sinking ship?'
I asked him. I wasn't particularly impressed by the story
because the world is full of legends of Nazi loot stashed
away here, there and everywhere. Some of them may be
true, but if they are *all* true, Germany would have ended
up with the whole of the government and most of the general
staff in South America.

Mr Mouse shrugged his shoulders. 'Roschmann didn't
know, it could have been anyone from Hitler down. The
man himself stayed, you understand, only packing cases

went.' Meuse hesitated. 'You have heard, I think, that during the war there were many attempts by Jews to actually buy their lives?'

I nodded.

'So. In Steszon, in Poland, there was a rich and influential Jewish community which literally denuded itself of possessions in an attempt to buy off the local military governor, General Schiller. They paid an estimated ten million pounds in cash, jewellery and works of art, all of which he succeeded in keeping for himself. It did nothing for them, of course, they went to the death camps anyway.' Meuse leaned forward. 'Mr Straun, Roschmann knew nothing of this, he knew only that General Schiller had a vast amount of wealth that he wished carried to a place of safety.'

'And where was that?' I asked.

'First here, for refuelling. One assumes there were German agents who would arrange that. What happened afterwards, Roschmann didn't know. Perhaps a rendezvous with a U-Boat. Perhaps—anything.'

I said, 'You are sure he doesn't know?'

Meuse nodded. 'Quite sure. The man is a little strange and his memory sketchy. You will understand that when they reached these waters they were sunk. Roschmann talks of a "great explosion", so one assumes they hit a mine. Whatever happened, he was the only one who survived and by a miracle reached the mainland more dead than alive. He was made a prisoner of war, his mind numb with shock. Only after years did some of his memory of the events of that night begin to return. But if what he says is true, the wreck of that torpedo boat is still in these waters somewhere, along with the Steszon treasure.'

My God, I thought, so that's where the Heavenly Twins come in. The IRA always needs money, and an apparently genuine search for an Armada galleon would cover a systematic search for the German wreck. But where had they picked up the trail? 'Tell me, Mr Meuse,' I said, 'supposing all this is true, why exactly are you here?'

'Always there are rumours of Nazi gold.' He spread his hands. 'So I come to Europe on business, they say, "Have a look while you are there. If there is anything, the locals will know. The locals always know."'

'And do they?' He was right about locals knowing, but are locals telling? Oh dear me, no.

Meuse smiled wryly. 'If they do, they are not telling. But there is one other thing.'

'Yes?'

'According to Roschmann, General Schiller wasn't any too sure of his own future under Hitler and intended following his money at the first opportunity.'

That was interesting. I asked, 'What made him think that?'

'Because along with the Steszon treasure there was a small boy, about three years old. He would have died in the explosion, of course.'

We looked at each other.

'Yes,' I said, 'of course.'

I was trying to imagine what the locals would say if they heard the news that the MacLiven of MacLiven was really the son of a Nazi general.

CHAPTER 11

I didn't see Chas till late the following morning, a relief really, when one isn't sure what to say. The man was so deep into being Scots that it seemed unthinkable to suggest he might be something else. Did it actually matter if he was somebody else? I walked along the cliff edge and wondered if Mr Mouse's story had been true. It had been late by the time I'd let him get to bed but his story had stayed the same. An odd little man but hard to shake. I wondered if I'd have done as well on someone else's remote island, being badgered by a local cop. Then I thought of Eichmann in his bullet-proof glass dock and the way the Israelis had got him there. They'd probably had eyes like big friendly dogs too, but I suggested that very few of them went out into the snow with little barrels of brandy round their necks.

When I got back there was no sign of Chas in the bar so I carried my drink out to the office, where Ailsa McCrae grudgingly informed me that the master and Miss Stewart were on the terrace.

'They went there for a bit of a talk, I'm thinking.'

Well, we policemen are a coarse lot and won't take a hint if it's dropped on our heads so I took my drink outside. The terrace was a stretch of gravel plus a few rustic benches behind the first tee and, as I walked round the corner, I could see the two of them, Chas sitting down and Kirstie standing, which is always a bad sign. I couldn't hear what was being said but it was the girl who was saying it, so I made crunchings on the path until they looked up and saw me. For a moment I thought she was going to tell me to go away but at the last moment she changed her mind, waved briefly and took herself off instead.

'Hi!' Chas said as I reached him. 'Let me buy you a drink.'

I showed him my full one. 'Saved you in the nick of time.'

'You're damn right you did.' Chas swallowed some of his own. He was still wearing those tartan trews, the top half of him in a conservatively plain scarlet windcheater. Over the years he'd always struck me as one of life's happy extroverts, which might not have been classic Scots but was very much genuine Chas, possibly not a Highlander's Highlander but at least one who got by pretty well in the country of his adoption. Chas had been a happy chap, as they say, but he wasn't all that happy now.

I sat down beside him. 'What's up with Kirstie?'

'Your guess is as good as mine.' Chas swirled whisky moodily round his glass. He said, 'I thought she liked it here.'

'Doesn't she?' Kirstie hadn't exactly welcomed me with open arms but it seemed to me she'd settled in the place well enough. Chas, too. Not every woman's choice, but she'd seemed happy enough with hers.

Chas said, 'She wants me to get shot of this place. Sell it or lease it and go back to the States.'

'With her?'

'Oh, sure. Says we can get married there.' He looked at me with troubled eyes. 'Any suggestions? I sold my place in Florida but that's no problem. It's—'

Chas was good at playing golf and being one of the boys, but in an odd way and in spite of his outrageous Harry Lauder Scottishness, he seemed to quite have the makings of a good hotelier, native canniness tending to benefit from American know-how. Too young to sit under an orange tree for the rest of his life.

'Do you *want* to go back?' I asked.

'Hell, no!' A good deal of the old Chas came back into his eyes. 'We were coming along fine, till this trouble began to louse things up.'

'So what made Kirstie change her mind?'

'What makes any woman change her mind?' He finished his drink and looked round as though hoping that the bar might have followed him out. It hadn't. He said, 'Funny, I really thought she *liked* it here. I mean, it's her own country, same as it is mine. Now she says I'm just making a fool of myself trying to run a hotel and that she's always wanted to live in the States—' His voice tailed off with the kind of hopeless query that seems built in with fifty-year-old men who fall in love with younger women. They may know they're making fools of themselves but that doesn't make it any easier to take.

We had lunch together and talked golf mainly. Amiable enough, but there was an undercurrent of something. Not against me particularly, but something. About 2.30 I made my excuses and pushed off, meaning to go to my room, only I came face to face with Mr Mouse who was coming down.

'Half an hour you're having free, Mr Straun?' He held out a hand so that I could see a 35 mm film cassette lying in the open palm. 'I'm on my way to develop a film.'

'Yes, can do.' I wondered what I was going to get. 'What are you going to use as a darkroom?'

'A darkroom. You're not reading the prospectus.' He quoted, ' "*Darkroom facilities are available for photography enthusiasts.*" '

I said apologetically, 'I forgot that bit. Handy, though.'

Meuse was leading me to the flight of steps that led to the dungeons. 'I am not expecting much,' he admitted. 'Two or three hours ago I ask the housekeeper if I can have it, but she says Miss Stewart has been using it and has the key. Apparently this is a nuisance because the old woman finds it convenient to store vacuum cleaners.' He sniffed in a rather spinsterish way. 'I tell you, dust is bad for darkrooms.'

'Yes,' I agreed, 'I can imagine. But you got the key in the end?'

He nodded. 'Miss Stewart says it's true about the cleaners.' He turned left before we'd gone far down the steps, and turned left again down a small corridor. There was a door at the end and, sure enough, a couple of commercial-sized Hoovers parked outside. One up to Kirstie, I thought. I hadn't known she was a hobbies girl but, since she was usually clutching a camera, I might have guessed.

Meuse pushed open the door and switched on the light. As a darkroom it was like the rest of the place, done up regardless. I wondered if Kirstie had had a hand in it but decided that it was more likely that Chas had simply given some professional his head. The room must have been some kind of store in days gone by, the size of a modern boxroom, now kitted out with fibreglass sink, a big Durst enlarger, hot plates and shelves of chemicals. There was even one of those rather fancy thermostatically controlled heaters that supply water at exactly the right temperature and keep on doing so without shifting more than half a degree either way.

'It could be worse,' Meuse said, which must have indicated relief from someone who must at least have been used to more space. He put the cassette on the white formica workbench and I saw it was Kodak Tri X.

'Black and white?' One gets so used to pictures of wildlife in colour.

Meuse nodded. 'Often black and white. I like the grain, you understand?'

'Yes.' Any schoolboy knew that much.

'That's why I use Tri X, I like to push a little.' He took a developing tank from a shelf and took out the reel and after a moment's search located the odds and ends of hardware that all users of darkrooms seem to need, then snapped out the light.

I asked, 'What is it you're going to show me, Mr Meuse?'

'Something I shot accidentally but fortunately, I think.' His voice in the darkness sounded pleased. 'I should have —I *hope* I have—at least one frame of poor Koch falling to his death. It is clear proof it was an accident.'

'Are you *sure*?'

Meuse's voice said, 'No, Mr Straun, I am not sure, because I was taking something else at the time. We must both be patient and wait.'

I leaned against the wall and waited. It seemed a long wait, but in fact he was pretty quick. Films are loaded in total darkness without even a red safelight to show you what you're doing. I remembered the loading of a length of tight wound film on to the developing tank's spiral as the well-nigh ultimate in fiddle, a struggle in the dark with a metre or so of film that went anywhere but the tiny grooves for which it was intended. But Mr Mouse seemed to have no problems. There was a pinging noise and a faint tinkle that I recognized as the end of the cassette being prised off and falling to the floor, a moment's pause while scissors snipped as he tidied up the leader, followed by brisk winding noises as the film did as it was told.

Meuse's voice said, 'So.'

I heard the spiral go 'clonk' in the tank and there was a second's silence before he said, 'Where's the damn light?'

'The cord's straight in front of you,' I told him.

He grunted in reply. It was not so much the reply of a man who can't be bothered to answer as the noise a man makes when he's been hit in the stomach. He grunted again and in the darkness a flailing foot smashed against my shin.

I said, 'What the hell—'

All at once the tiny room seemed packed with frenzied movement and a terrible rhythmical sound as though someone was being beaten to death with a mechanical hammer. There is something frighteningly elemental about things that happen in the dark, so that common sense is driven out in a blind panic for light. If I thought anything in those few seconds, it was that Meuse was having some kind of fit, then I'd jumped sideways out of range of that thrashing body and wrenched open the door. There was a glare that made me blink, then the door had swung wide and I turned to see Meuse thrown up in sharp relief as light from the fluorescents in the corridor poured in on him, a panting figure that jerked and twisted to 240 volts of alternating current that flowed into him from the hand gripped round the chrome tap of the water-heater.

Instinct can be a killer, and if I'd grabbed Meuse and tried to pull him off, the shock would simply have gone through me as well. Fortunately civilization has rubbed a good deal of nature's gifts off urban man and I never even began to reach for Mr Mouse, particularly as there was a large master switch set in the wall beside the heater. I knocked it up smartish and he collapsed on the floor as though the thing had suddenly dropped him, which I suppose in a way it had.

I said, 'Meuse!'

At that moment it would have made little difference what I'd said because his eyes were closed and his lips were blue. I dropped on my knees beside him. Close up, he looked even worse and if he was breathing at all, I could see no sign of it. I glanced over my shoulder with some kind of hope that a couple of doctors might be looking in on me, but all I could see was the brickwork on the other side of the corridor. It's not fair, I thought, the poor little bastard isn't even German.

That didn't get any response either, so I stretched him out and got busy with what I remembered about resuscitation.

All in all it was a busy half-hour but successful. Rather to my surprise I'd got Meuse breathing again sufficiently steadily for me to leave him and run upstairs for help. If there'd been a doctor among the guests it would have been handy, but there wasn't, though as luck would have it some nice woman answered my rather desperate appeals with the news that she'd been a hospital sister before she married, and proceeded to cope accordingly.

She was pretty good and under her direction we got Meuse to bed, looking if anything rather better than Chas, who was taking it badly.

'For Chrissake, Angus, what gives in this madhouse? You were there—how did he do it? Kirstie was using the photographic gear herself this morning and it worked OK.'

'It must have been some kind of fault in the wiring.'

'In the *wiring*? The wiring's new!'

I said, 'Take it easy, Chas, Mrs Mason says Meuse will be all right. We'll sort the rest out later.'

Well, if we were lucky we would. Mr Mouse's misfortune was creating a nice little excitement and I had the feeling that some of the guests had never had so much fun in years, so I left them to it and went back to the darkroom. I'd locked the door behind me when I'd left and I let myself in and locked it behind me again. In an excess of caution, I'd been carrying the developing tank around with me and I put it on the bench with a feeling of relief. Maybe I was unduly suspicious but I'd have hated anything to have happened to the film inside it.

'Oh Mr Mouse,' I said to the shelves of photographic gear, 'you really should have stayed in Israel.'

The gear didn't say anything sensible back, but I noticed that whoever had planned the darkroom had thrown in a pair of rubber gloves. I put them on and gave my attention to the water-heater. What had happened was pretty clear, because the pull-cord that worked the safety light was not far left of the heater's mixer tap. With his film safely in the developing tank, Meuse must have reached out in the dark to turn on the light and got hold of the water tap instead.

But why had it been live?

I had a look. There was a fair amount of wiring behind it, as there usually is in darkrooms—leads to dish warmers and enlargers and lights of one sort or another. One was freshly taped close to the mounting of the water-heater but it looked safe enough. I wondered how long that insulating tape had been there. Difficult to tell—an hour, a month, who was to say? I switched the heater on cautiously. Nothing startling happened, but then nothing was likely to unless I touched the damn thing, so I took the plug off the light box and peeled the blue and brown leads apart enough to twist the line conductor round the tap and earth the other to the metal outlet of the sink. Nothing lit up.

A practical demonstration, gentlemen, is worth a great deal of theory. Who had said that? Some long-forgotten instructor on some equally long-forgotten course. Dead right he'd been, all the same. I fiddled around a bit more and in the end took off my rubber gloves and cautiously applied the tip of my finger to the tap in such a way that any jolt of current would throw me off. A bloody silly thing to do, but I was gripped by a certainty that the thing was perfectly safe. I was right, too. Someone had wired the heater up to the mains with what the book calls malicious intent. Someone had opened a locked door while I'd been cosseting Mr Mouse and unwired it. Oh well.

I made up a brew of Acuspeed and sloshed it into the tank, set the stop clock on the wall to nine minutes and hung around, inverting the thing every now and then. Meuse had said he'd pushed the film a bit, which probably meant he'd rated it at treble the usual speed to bring out the grain. Well, the developer I was using would see to that. I watched the clock, kept the solution on the move and wished I'd had the guts to go on smoking cigarettes. A lot of the time, not smoking didn't matter, but part of the time it mattered very much. Who was I kidding, it mattered all the time. I emptied out the developer and replaced it with fixer. Emptied that and gave it five minutes wash, then pulled the strip of film out and had a look.

Thirty-five millimetre is a pretty small negative to study at the best of times and just about useless if you're after detail, so I dried the strip off and stuck it in the enlarger. I didn't have to worry about which frames to select because Meuse seemed to have exposed only two, but they were enough. I stood staring down at the bright, ten-by-eight image on the baseboard and mentally gave him best. If anyone had pushed Luther to his death, it certainly hadn't been Meuse because he'd been otherwise engaged at the time, taking a picture that showed some kind of bird sitting smugly in the foreground while in the background the figure of a man fell like a rag doll down the face of a sheer cliff.

I looked at the picture for a long time, trying to make sense of the negative image. After a while I raised the head of the enlarger and refocused the picture to twice its previous size. It was hard to tell, because the top of the cliff had been shrouded in mist. Just the same, there was an outline of something up there. Like the figure of someone standing on the edge, frozen by the camera, with one arm still outstretched.

CHAPTER 12

The golf clubhouse at Ardrossan was a single-storeyed granite-walled affair that looked like something that had been built for coastal defence during the Napoleonic Wars. In the morning sunlight it looked clean and strong and functional, cut in there against the side of the hill. Stand with your back to the entrance and straight ahead was the sea, put yourself at a right angle and you faced the ridge that hid the crofts of Gavin Grant's lost dream. The trouble was, it hadn't been his own dream, though that was his problem, not mine.

You can find golf clubs in Scotland that are unlike any-thing else in the world. At Arisaig they used to put barbed wire round the greens to keep the sheep out and you had to chip over it before you could putt. Ardrossan gave the impression of being fashioned from a series of heather-covered humps on which greens had been made, with stretches of impenetrable wilderness in between. Nevertheless, what greens I could see were immaculate and the granite chippings covering the tiny car park had apparently been freshly raked.

I looked at my watch and saw it was still only five to ten, so I took myself in search of the Pro's shop to make sure I'd paid my green fee before the Reverend Grant arrived. To an outside observer it might have seemed that I had other things to do that morning than keeping a golf appointment, but for once it was not just the golf. I badly needed an excuse to talk to Gavin Grant.

There was a kind of bothy behind the clubhouse where a raw-boned figure in ancient tweeds stood at a workbench winding new whipping on what appeared to be an equally ancient driver. There were a few sets of clubs leaning against the walls along with a sepia-toned photograph or two. Golf circa World War One.

'Good mornin', sor. Are ye lookin' for a game?' *G. W. Brodie: Professional* was over the door. G. W. Brodie was studying me with a keen eye. 'There's na many gentlemen about as yet.'

'I'm having a round with Mr Grant,' I told him. 'Perhaps you'd take my green fee while I'm waiting.'

'Aye, I'll do that.'

I gave him the five pounds he asked for and decided that at that rate Ardrossan must have some remarkably generous members. On the strength of it I bought three balls.

'Ha' a fine round,' Brodie wished me. He added, 'The gentleman was a handy player in his day.'

'Weren't we all?' I said. I found it hard to picture Gavin Grant as the kind of player someone like G. W. Brodie would describe as 'handy', but then one never knew with this game. I gave him an appreciative look. 'What does he play to?'

'Och, the poor man's back to fifteen.' Brodie's eagle eyes dropped to my bag, left over from other days. So were the clubs, for that matter. A gift at the time, and just as well, too. 'And yourself, now?'

'About six,' I said.

'That'll be on account of your arm, I'm thinking.' Brodie took my 7 iron from the bag and, with a large duster, removed a trace of mud.

'Possibly.' I'd been carrying the clubs on my left shoulder, so how had he known? I'd have liked to have asked him this and that about Gavin Grant but it wouldn't have been fair, and in any case he wouldn't have told me. So I said something about it being quiet for the time of year.

'Quieter than it should be,' Brodie said. He hesitated, then presumably decided that this was no breaking of confidence. 'The gentlemen have no been so keen to play here since the strangers came.' He jerked his head in the direction the crofts lay. I liked the 'strangers' bit.

I unwrapped a ball and dropped the plastic in the old biscuit tin provided. The tin must have been something of an antique in its own right. 'Do they cause you much trouble?'

The barest of pauses. 'Not so that you'd notice.'

Which would be as far as I'd get. Beyond the club house, wheels crunched to a stop and a door slammed. Two doors? I picked up my bag and went out to meet my opponent.

'Good morning, Straun.'

'Good morning, sir.' Fewer people to 'sir' to as the years go by, but no awkwardness here, one of those time warps to gentler days. And the old boy looked unexpectedly spry in cords and an old but clean windcheater, brighter-eyed than at our last meeting, as though he kept a special outdoor model of himself for these occasions. And yet there was something. Furtive? No, the Gavin Grants of this world aren't furtive by nature, but quite undoubtedly something.

'I've brought a caddie. Hope you don't mind. Gettin' old.'

'Of course not.' But I'd spotted the caddie, him not being the kind of chap one could miss. Sandals, jeans and a beard, plus one of those bands round his head, one of the middle-aged drop-out brigade. I looked at him and he looked at me. Oddly, come to think of it. Not Beastly Basil from the cliffs that day, but vaguely familiar. I didn't talk to him, possibly because he had a sort of cocky look that didn't go with the role, quite apart from the fact that I can't do with caddies who pull trolleys, Kirstie Stewart excepted.

Grant was looking at what we could see of the course with the appreciation of someone who would rather play golf than do most things. 'We seem to have the place much to ourselves,' he was saying. 'We really are most fortunate.'

According to the professional, we'd have been singularly unfortunate to find the place crowded, but that was neither here nor there. We bickered over the honour and got him away first, thanks to this and that. The first hole, according to the scoreboard, was two hundred and fifty yards, on the face of it a short par 4 but with a good hundred and fifty yards of thick bracken that had to be carried in order to reach the token fairway that rambled towards a raised and heavily bunkered green. It was something one got either right or horribly, horribly wrong.

'A nice wee hole,' the Reverend Grant said. He took a 2 wood from the battered bag his dreadful attendant held out and waggled it lovingly. In truth, it was less a 2 wood than a brassie. For a moment I'd even thought that it boasted a hickory shaft but a second look showed it to be brown painted metal, but you have to go back a fair way for one of those. I half expected him to go the whole hog and balance his ball on a little pile of sand but at the last moment he produced a tee, lined himself up and drove.

'A very nice one,' I said. And my word, I meant it. I'd
no idea where the ball was going but the old chap's swing
was something to treasure, the kind of thing one catches
occasionally in old sepia photographs of the great days long
gone. Judged against today's state of the art, he ended up
looking almost as though he was about to run after the ball
instead of trying to look like a Roman Candle. It was a style
that dated back at least a generation earlier, but presumably
Gavin Grant had been schooled by one of the old breed and
never been exposed to new-fangled ideas since. Old-
fashioned or not, there was a fluidity and naturalness about
the man's drive that made it a thing of beauty, and when I
got around to spotting his ball I wasn't surprised to find it
a short pitch from the green and dead centre between two
bunkers. A well-nigh perfect shot.

'There's no wind,' Grant observed, apologetically I
thought. 'The ball's flying remarkably true.'

Well, of course it depends how you hit it. I couldn't see
any point in showing how clever I was so I took a 2 wood
likewise and socked one hard enough to have found the
green if the left-hand bunker hadn't got there first.

'My dear sir,' Grant said, 'that was poor luck. You
deserved better.'

I said, 'I should have hit it better.' But for the first one
of the day it could have been worse.

By and large it was an interesting hole. I got out of the
sand adequately and two putted for my par, while my
opponent chipped to within five feet of the flag before
producing a venerable wooden-shafted putter to hole un-
hesitatingly for a birdie.

'My word,' Grant said, 'I did enjoy that!'

'I'm not surprised,' I told him. 'I enjoy birdies, too. The
trouble is they don't come up as often as they used to.'

'Good heavens, I didn't mean the score!' Gavin Grant
looked faintly shocked. There was a curiously touching

naïvety about the man that made it clear that he really
hadn't been thinking of his birdie. Sad, really, that so many
years of listening to gamesmanship between holes should
make me doubt him.

'No?' So if he didn't mean the score, what did he mean?

He looked at me almost shyly. 'It's just that it's so
enjoyable to be playing *against* somebody again.'

We were at the second tee. Par 3 one hundred and
sixty-four yards. 'The Colonel's'—whoever the colonel had
been. I made my voice a lot more surprised than I felt as I
said, 'You play a good deal on your own?'

Flower Power pushed himself between us, a club in his
hand, holding it out to Grant. 'You want a 5 for this.'

The old boy took it meekly. 'Thank you, Dave.'

I looked at Dave, the sort of look that was meant to
indicate he should withdraw and leave the tee to his betters,
a ploy that proved outstandingly unsuccessful. 'Blank eyes'
people say, when they're trying to describe their particular
bogey man, conjuring up a world crawling with blank-eyed
homicidal maniacs and rapists. Dave didn't have blank
eyes. Bright, yes. Pig-like, certainly. One is apt to say 'full
of low cunning' when referring to people one doesn't like,
and I certainly didn't like Dave, but in fairness he struck
me as being pretty intelligent.

I said again, 'You play a good deal on your own?'

Dave hadn't moved. Grant took the 5 iron and simply
nodded. I thought his swing might not be quite as good this
time but I was mistaken, because it was just as good and
he found the green about ten feet from the hole. Maybe he
didn't see much of other people but it looked as though he
played a hell of a lot on his own.

We halved that hole and to my relief I won the next. We
chatted of this and that but it was curiously difficult with
Dave hauling his trolley between us rather as though we
were towing him on a piece of string. If Grant had been

some kind of high-class London villain, I'd have said he'd brought his minder along.

'The fourth is really rather pretty,' Grant said.

He was right. You played up a narrow fairway to a burn that splashed down a hillside. Once over the water the hole seemed to dog-leg round some trees, hard to plot because the sun was making dark shadows at their feet. Half-a-dozen seagulls wheeling overhead and the white tail of a rabbit bouncing away as we moved. Maybe it was a bit like the kind of hole they'd have had in *Brigadoon* but it was quite a sight for all that.

We both drove our balls to around the area of the turn, mine the back one, caught by the rough. As we reached it I said, 'Is the club short of members, you find it hard to fix up games?'

'He likes playing alone,' Dave said.

Grant had been trying to spot his own ball. 'Go on ahead and look,' I said. And then, as he set off in his slightly other-worldly fashion, I stepped in front of Dave the caddie. 'Not you.'

'Why not me, dad?' He was older than me if anything, but like I said, for some people time stands still.

'Because I wanted to have a quiet word,' I told him civilly. 'You interrupt when Mr Grant and I are speaking. You get in the way. Don't.'

Dave studied me with those too-close-together eyes of his, then without haste he withdrew his right hand from the pocket of his jeans and held it up so that I could admire the way his brass knuckleduster shone in the sunshine. 'How about these in your teeth, man?' he inquired conversationally.

I trod on his toes.

Toes, like fingers, are extraordinarily sensitive extremities and Dave's were bare apart from the straps of his scruffy sandals. At first his reaction was disappointing because for a second or two he didn't move, but then his eyes opened wide and he made a noise not unlike a sigh, probably because he was finding it hard to believe that the pain was real. His bad luck that I've never taken to the modern summer golf shoe with ribbed rubber soles. A full set of old-fashioned steel studs for me every time.

'Jesus, man—' Dave grabbed the front of my jacket more in desperation than anything else, so I took hold of his grubby thumb and bent it back to somewhere approaching the point of no return.

'Keep your voice down,' I said, 'or I'll break it.'

The sudden fear in the wretched man's eyes should have been gratifying but in point of fact I found it rather shaming, something I did my best to hide. I said, 'Listen, you poor sad bastard, I am a police officer and if you don't go away—*right* away—I shall arrest you on some trumped-up charge and have a couple of the heavy squad work you over in the roughest possible way. It wouldn't surprise me if we found some prohibited drugs on you, too.'

For a moment indignation overcame pain. 'I haven't—'

'There's plenty of time.'

Dave accepted the situation. He shrugged, said, 'Oh shit —' and turned to limp his way back to the club house. It confirmed what I'd noticed before, that at least some of the people who whinge about police brutality actually believe it. Just to show I meant business I called after him, 'What's your name?'

'Dave. Dave Smith.'

Well it was a common enough name, so maybe a coincidence. 'You haven't a brother who's an antique dealer in Islington by any chance?' God, he'd hesitated! 'Come on, don't fool about. I can check.'

'Yes.' Reluctantly. But of course. Smith had been near enough in Walker's gallery to hear Chas telling me to catch that particular train. So that was how word had got around.

And with my picture and bomb squad story in the papers, what a word it was. I could just picture the Heavenly Twins turning their thumbs down on the idea of my arrival.

'All right,' I said. 'Blow.'

He blew.

From fifty yards ahead Grant called back queryingly. I caught the word, 'Dave'.

I grabbed the handle of his now abandoned trolley and trudged on to join him. 'Dave didn't feel too good,' I said.

'Oh.' Grant stared past me at the distant figure. 'He seems to be limping.'

'Yes.' I nodded at the trolley. 'Look, can you manage this?'

'My dear Straun, of course!' The fierce pride of the elderly when their strength is in question. Though in all fairness, anyone who could hit a ball like Gavin Grant could probably tow a few clubs behind him without difficulty.

I said, 'If you can manage on your own, I'm surprised you put up with him.'

'I—' Grant started to speak, then changed his mind. Finally he said, 'He likes to make himself useful.'

'The man's a thug,' I told him. 'He hasn't the slightest intention of being useful. He simply doesn't want you to be alone with me. Come to that, he probably doesn't want you chatting privately to anyone.'

I found myself comparing him with the late departed Dave, and in that moment whatever it was that for the past hour had been lurking at the bottom of my memory came to the surface with a rush. Of course I'd seen Dave before. He was the scruffy character I'd noticed eating alongside the nuns in the London to Edinburgh train.

It took a moment for the full implication of that to sink in. All right, *someone* had pushed me out of that train, but I certainly hadn't seen who did it. I'd assumed it had been the compulsive talker who'd latched on to me from the table

opposite mine in the restaurant car for no better reason than
that we'd been in conversation a few minutes before. But
suppose as I looked out of that window he'd walked on and
Dave had come up? True, there was no reason for supposing
that Dave had any reason to murder me either, but just
suppose—

Grant's gentle voice broke in on my thoughts.

'Come, Straun, I can't have you saying things like that.'
He was looking at me reproachfully, but not that reproachfully. Sit-com parson he might look, but there was something
in the old man's gentle face that I found faintly disturbing.
Guilt? Fear?

'Look,' I said, 'suppose we sit down and you tell me a
few things without Dave or anyone else listening in.' I led
the old boy to a bank and sat him down. 'It's true, isn't it?
These—protégés of yours, they make sure you don't play
with other members?'

He smiled a little wistfully. 'It isn't really necessary, I'm
afraid. Feeling against the commune has always been rather
strong and has been getting even stronger of late. Not
unnaturally the members hold me responsible, so I'm
hardly a sought-after partner.'

'But the first time we met. You had another of your
"crofters" hanging about then.'

Grant dropped his eyes, rather like a guilty schoolboy.
'Well, yes, I suppose I had.'

I said, 'And he was hanging about just to make sure you
didn't tell me about the *Santa Marina*?'

Grant looked at me pleadingly. 'My dear fellow, I beg of
you—'

'It's all right,' I told him. His fear was uncomfortably
real. 'There's nobody here besides the two of us. Tell me
about it. Tell me why you said the *Santa Marina* was wrecked
off this coast when you know perfectly well she got back to
Cadiz.'

An old Canberra moaned overhead and headed out to sea, seeking out the next day's weather. We watched its wings rocking gently as they hit the colder air. A couple more moments of left-behind sound, hammered down at us like some kind of celestial reminder that the Armada was long gone.

Perhaps something of the same idea occurred to Grant, because he asked suddenly, 'How did you find out?' The curious arrogance of the specialist who so often imagines all knowledge of his subject is exclusive to him.

'It's on record, and it's easy enough to look up,' I told him. And then, when he didn't answer, I went on, 'Would you like to tell me what happened?'

'They gave me something.'

'Gave you what?'

Grant made a gesture as though brushing away the memory of something distasteful. 'Some drug. As a joke, you know.' He turned to me suddenly and some of his diffidence seemed to have dropped away from him, as though he was realizing for the first time that he really was free to talk. He said, 'Of course I'd known for some time that some members of the Community made use of them but I hadn't paid much attention to it. Young people are always experimenting with something, aren't they?'

'Yes,' I said. 'So they tell me. Do you know what they gave you?'

He shook his head. 'It was at some gathering they'd invited me to. Not that I particularly wanted to go but one doesn't like to say no on these occasions.'

I pictured the unworldly Gavin Grant as the unwilling guest of the freaks for whom he'd provided a haven.

'All right,' I said, 'your young friends gave you some kind of drug. Then what happened?'

'I remembered.'

I said, 'Tell me what you remembered,' and after a while
he did.

I could have guessed the background of what he had to
tell me, the happy, indulged childhood spent largely abroad
with well-to-do parents. Then Cambridge, a call to the
Church, oddly unconvincing it seemed to me, but then, how
does one describe a spiritual experience? Perhaps he felt it
was none of my business, but at least I gathered that the
war had come soon after he'd taken orders and he'd tried
to join one of the services as a chaplain but the medical
boards turned him down. Eventually, in 1943, his calling
had brought him to Ardrossan.

'You know,' Grant told me, 'I liked Ardrossan. I liked
the place and the people, although goodness knows there
weren't many of them. But of course, as so often happens
up here, they were spread over a considerable area, so I
travelled a lot. I got to know the MacLiven of those days
pretty well—on one Sunday a month he'd send a boat over
for me and I'd hold a service out there.'

Grant fiddled with the grip of the club he was holding.
'That's how I came to be there at the time of the last big
tide. You've heard of the Day of Wrath?'

I nodded.

'It swept so many away. I did what little I could but I
was nearly drowned myself when my head struck a rock.'
He paused. 'So they tell me.'

'You don't remember?'

He smiled that gently deprecating smile that some people
acquire along with a disability. Then he shook his head.
'No, I'm afraid not. I was ill for quite a time, you see, and
when I got about again there were things that had happened
quite a short time before that I couldn't remember. Gone
for good. At least I thought so, until that silly business with
the young people. It seems I remembered all sorts of things
when I was—under the influence, I suppose one should

say. But of course when the effects wore off I'd forgotten it all again.'

'You mean you *still* don't remember?' I hadn't catered for this.

Grant said apologetically, 'No, I'm afraid not.'

I said, 'Then if it's not a rude question, how do you know you ever did remember anything?'

'Because they told me.'

'Your *Crofters* told you?' It would have been easier to say 'your drug-crazed, layabout, ageing hippies' but there was no point in upsetting him. 'Why should they do that?'

'I imagine in the hope that I might remember still more.' He smiled indulgently. 'Alas, they were disappointed.'

'Alas indeed,' I agreed. The pure in heart can be excessively tiresome on occasion. 'What exactly was it you were supposed to have remembered?

'It was about a boat. A German boat of some kind, carrying a lot of valuables.'

So Roschmann's story had been true after all. I sat on the short grass, fiddling with my putter, watching a couple of young rabbits chasing each other on the far side of the fairway. I wondered how the Heavenly Twins had got into the act, but as it happened I didn't have to wonder for long.

'Do you know,' I asked, 'what kind of valuables? Where they came from, for instance?'

Grant looked puzzled and shook his head. 'I really don't know what *sort* of valuables. But they were lost, whatever they were, because Robert MacLiven and his men managed to sink the boat. That was why—David and his friends decided they'd go in search of it. They knew nothing of diving, of course, but David had lived in Ireland for a time and knew the Donovan brothers, so he wrote to them and they came over.' Grant paused, as though realizing for the first time his own involvement. 'The Donovans tried to make it look as though they were diving for an old galleon so that it would throw people off the scent. And I, God forgive me, helped in the deception.'

He looked sad and old and tired and I hadn't the heart to press him further.

I got to my feet. 'Forget it,' I said. 'Let's get on with the game.'

He beat me in the end. His handicap helped, I suppose, but then that's what handicaps are for, and he played the hell of a good game. Afterwards I said I'd go back home with him for a dram, which was really only another way of saying I'd see him safely to the door. I didn't think the dreaded Dave was likely to take it out of the old boy but one never knows, so we bounced our way over the appalling roads to Grant's place, a peaceful, square, two-storeyed stone building with not a Crofter in sight.

'What a grand day it's been,' Grant said as he led the way in. He seemed to be in a state of euphoria, which I suppose was hardly surprising if he only got to play with a fellow human being once every year or so. He led the way to his study, a cosy shambles of dusty furniture and walls covered in old sepia photographs and left me there while he went in search of a bottle. When he got back I was studying a picture of a whole group of his poor rescued souls, looking to my prejudiced mind like a particularly depraved version of *The Pirates of Penzance*.

I asked, 'How did you come to start—well, helping these people?' It was a difficult question to phrase without giving offence.

'There were just a few to start with.' For a moment it looked as though he wasn't sure himself how it had all started. 'They seemed so desperate for some kind of roots, you know, and I had this land doing nothing. It seemed wrong not to help them, so I let them stay.'

'And the others?'

He said diffidently, 'They just came.'

I bet they did, I thought. I took the drink he gave me and sipped the smoky malt. Grant seemed to have had a thing about Crofter groups, they stared out of the frames like weird old school photographs, and I stared back, because the things had got a certain horrible fascination. Then I jumped. Jammed between a couple of ageing thugs a girl looked blankly into the camera, straight-haired, expressionless, in a shapeless sack of a dress. She looked like the wrath of God but there was something vaguely familiar about her.

'What is it?' Grant asked.

I shook my head. 'Nothing.' But the penny had dropped. Do the drab's hair and put her in a decent dress and she'd be a different girl. In fact, she'd be Kirstie Stewart.

CHAPTER 13

It was a rough, rudimentary road, its surface covered with granite chippings that must have done no good at all to the local tyres. On the outskirts of the village the grey, uncompromising rectangle of St Andrew's Church momentarily blocked the view and I braked with a suddenness that would have been disastrous had there been any traffic. Idle curiosity it might be, but in a lean season an answer to any question at all is worth having. I walked up to the massive door and gave it a push. Had it been locked, I don't suppose I'd have bothered to discover who held the key, but apparently people didn't knock off the church plate in these parts and the door creaked open.

A notice just inside read: *Please keep door closed because of birds.*

I did as I was told and looked around me in the dim light. Unless you're an expert, the parish churches of Scotland are not easy to date because they all look much the same.

Enthusiasts talk about the beauty of their simplicity, but to me St Andrew's was bleak and forbidding. A few flowers might have helped but the only ones in sight had been dead a long time, like the mummified sparrow that must have got in one day when the door was open. I shivered a little and started my search for the list of incumbents. It turned out to be behind the door, white paint on black board, rather carefully done. Not many in those long-lived parts, the first a David Mackintosh, 1724–46, the last someone, curiously, with the same name who'd arrived in 1980 and was presumably still going strong. I raised my eyes to the war years and suddenly it wasn't just idle curiosity any more.

> 1935 Rev. P. D. H. Munroe
> 1950 Rev. A. Masters, MC

I studied the inscription carefully but the spacing between the two names was the same as for all the others, the paint original and uncorrected. Literally in black and white was the statement that the Rev. P. D. H. Munroe had not only come to Ardrossan four years before the war but had still been ministering to the local flock five years after it.

So where had the Reverend Gavin Grant come in?

I stared through the lead grey glass of the nearest window and took in a granite headstone, leaning at an angle of about forty-five degrees to its owner. I supposed the wind had pushed it there, along with the trees and everything else remotely movable. Surprising, really, that the church itself hadn't moved. But suddenly I was no longer surprised about Gavin Grant. I went out and shut the door carefully behind me.

I'd borrowed Chas's boat for the day, and when I got back Kirstie was coming down to the quay to meet me. I had a nasty moment thinking that something had happened to Meuse but he was apparently tougher than I'd thought.

'Oh, Mr Mouse is fine!' she said in answer to my question. 'He wants to get up, only Mrs Mason won't let him.' We walked together in silence for a few minutes while she got around to asking the question she must have come for. 'Did you have a good day with Grant and his friends?'

'You must know a good deal more about his friends than I do,' I told her. 'Suppose you tell me about the lot of you.'

She was silent for a moment, then she shrugged her shoulders and said philosophically, 'Well, I suppose someone was bound to get around to it sooner or later. How did you find out?'

'It wasn't all that difficult. Grant's got a sort of class group of you on the wall.'

'Oh no! Not really!' Kirstie's voice went up a tone. Then she sighed and said resignedly, 'I suppose it's in his study. It never occurred to me he was going to hang the bloody thing up.' She added, 'I was never really one of them, you know.'

'What were you doing there, then? Trying to get a story?' I'd almost forgotten she'd worked on a newspaper.

'That was the general idea.'

'Judging from the picture,' I said, 'you were made for the part.'

Kirstie laughed uncertainly. 'It's not terribly difficult, the dressing up bit. They're so *weird* that you don't really have to worry about going over the top. I got this idea after I'd been reading about the New Crofters and my editor thought it might make a good feature, so I just went ahead. Getting the clothes was easy—I picked the lot up at a village jumble sale. After that it was just a matter of getting myself a bit grubby and I was in.'

'Just like that? No introduction?'

'No, I just turned up.' Kirstie paused. 'Have you ever had anything to do with—well, that kind of people?'

I shook my head. 'No. Only at a distance.'

'They're curiously innocent. They're so anxious not to be thrown by anything that they'll accept just about any story without checking if it's true.' She pushed back her hair impatiently. 'I told them that the friend I'd been travelling with had got into trouble with the police and so I was on my own. It must have sounded terribly normal to them, so they let me stay.'

I said, 'Didn't they ask about your camera?'

'Oh yes. I told them I'd stolen it.'

Well, it was practical, I supposed. In her place I'd probably have spent hours concocting some yarn that was infinitely more complicated that wouldn't have answered half as well. 'So you had your camera,' I said, 'and all the story you wanted. Why didn't you write it?'

She frowned. 'How do you know I didn't?'

'I checked.'

'I felt sorry for Grant, I suppose.' We'd reached the top of the path. Kirstie sat down on the short turf and hugged her knees, and after a while I dropped down beside her. Not for the first time, I found myself exploring the not particularly novel paradox of how one man could be attracted to two vastly different women. Laurie and Kirstie didn't even look alike, as though that had anything to do with it. But it was Kirstie who was sitting beside me, shredding a daisy now, that sure sign of ill ease.

Finally she said softly, 'Damn you, Straun, why can't you just forget the whole thing! It's none of your business.'

'I suppose,' I said, 'because you said much the same thing the first day we met, and I wondered why.' I stretched out beside her, more because it was comfortable than to give her confidence. But yes, that too. 'Look,' I said, 'poor old Grant told me about the joke with the drugs. And I suppose I've got it right if I suppose you were there?' I left it for a moment but she didn't answer. 'Be reasonable, Kirstie,' I said, 'don't fool about. This is important.'

She looked at me. Her green eyes seemed huge in that small face, full of an appeal I couldn't understand. 'All right,' she said at last, 'I was there, along with Dave and a few others. But I didn't give him anything. As a matter of fact, I don't even know for sure what it was, or why they gave it to him at all. Except that it's the kind of mindless thing they think is funny. Like making a dog drunk.'

'So what did happen?'

'He started talking about the war—about something that had happened here. He doesn't remember a thing about it all the rest of the time, but I expect you knew that?' She looked at me queryingly.

I nodded. 'What did he have to say about the boat?'

'Oh, you know about that?' Kirstie tugged a tuft of grass out and tossed it idly into the air, where the wind caught it and scattered it. She went on, 'He didn't seem to know a great deal. Just that some Nazi with cold feet had loaded up a boat with loot and tried to get it out of Germany. Only by some mischance it turned up here.'

'What else did Grant say?'

'That—that was all.' I suppose she sensed that I didn't believe her because she went on defensively. 'He just rambled on a bit but there was nothing that made sense.'

'Like hell there was nothing,' I told her. 'That boat didn't come here by accident. No Nazi general would have loaded up with goodies and then just sent it off to an enemy coast hoping for the best. There must have been some kind of welcoming committee. So tell me about that.'

Kirstie said quietly, 'Oh, why won't you believe me when I say I don't know?'

'Because we both know it isn't true.' I pulled her round until she faced me. 'Don't be a fool, Kirstie. You've been trying to get rid of me ever since I arrived because you're scared stiff I'm going to rake up something that's best left alone. Like a skeleton in the MacLiven cupboard you don't want the world to know about.' The expression on her face didn't change and suddenly the penny dropped. '*Or one you don't want Chas to know about.*'

Her head spun round and for a moment those extraordinary green eyes grew even wider and if she'd had a meat cleaver ready to hand I'd have been getting ready to jump. But there was no meat cleaver, and anyway she wasn't that sort of girl. After a while she said in a low voice, 'Does he really have to know?'

'That Dad was guilty of giving aid and comfort to the enemy, or whatever they call it?'

'He wasn't,' Kirstie said. 'But I suppose it must have looked like that. No smoke without fire, that sort of thing. Only it's not just that—'

I said reasonably, 'If this all came out in front of Dave and his crew, what's the secrecy anyway?'

'Because he came to it later. After the boat bit. And I suppose by that time whatever they'd given him had gone even deeper and he'd gone back to speaking Gaelic. The Crofters don't know it, of course, but I do.' She hesitated. 'His Gaelic is more Irish than Scots, by the way. I suppose Gavin Grant could be Irish himself. Not that it matters.'

Apart from the fact that it would make him at least sympathetic to the Heavenly Twins, I thought, the ethnic bit being strong in old Ireland. 'So?' I said.

'So Robbie MacLiven lived in Berlin before the war. Did you know that?'

'No. Doing what?' I hadn't been prepared for a business tycoon MacLiven.

'He painted.'

'Did he now?' One didn't imagine Scottish lairds as painters either, but why not? I remembered the rather striking abstracts hung unobtrusively in the castle. If not his, presumably his choice. 'I wonder why he chose Germany instead of France or Italy.'

'He was educated at Heidelberg,' Kirstie said, 'so I suppose he just liked the place—the people, too. But by 1939 he knew there was going to be a war. I gather he stayed on till the last minute, hoping for the best, but in the end it was a choice between being interned and coming home. So he came home.' Considering she had heard the original in drug-induced Gaelic, she was making the story rational enough.

'Go on,' I said.

'Robbie MacLiven came back here to live and nobody seems to have worried much about his German background. Apparently he had some kind of chest trouble so there was no question of him serving in the forces. He looked after his land and served on local committees and so on until one day in 1943 he got a message to the effect that he was known to be a good friend of Germany and the Fatherland needed his help. Nothing dangerous, nothing that would harm his own countrymen. All Robert MacLiven had to do was to give a small boat seizure berth for twelve hours at the most. In payment for this service the boat's commander would return Robert MacLiven's son.'

'His *son*?' The boat was not altogether news but a son most definitely was. 'You mean he had a wife, too?'

Kirstie shook her head. 'No, he had a child by some girl who apparently wasn't free to marry him. When Robert was hustled back to Scotland in 1939 she and the child were on the other side of Germany. He couldn't get in touch with her and he couldn't stay, so that was that. He never saw her again.'

'And Robbie really believed that they'd give him the boy back?' I saw where the story was going and didn't like it all that much. So easy to believe what we want to believe. And yet Roschmann had spoken of a small boy, too.

Kirstie was shaking her head. 'No, he didn't believe them. Robbie had spent too long in Germany not to have his sources of information, and he'd already heard that the child and his mother had died in a concentration camp, which meant the Nazis were having him on, pushing him into the arrangement, knowing that he wouldn't find he'd been tricked until it was too late to back out. The classic double-cross.' She smiled briefly. 'Two can play at that game. Apparently Robbie sent back a message to say that he agreed to the proposals and gave them a course between the islands to what he promised was a safe berth. Then he loaded it with explosive and when the boat eventually arrived he blew it up.'

It was a good story, and it had a ring of truth about it because it was exactly the kind of game feuding clans had played on each other for centuries. The history of the Highlands is stiff with treachery and counter-treachery and whoever the German was who'd thought he could pull a Scot's leg to that extent simply didn't know his people. 'So what happened after that?' I asked.

'It seems none of the boat's crew survived,' Kirstie said. 'But the next day a small boy was discovered on a beach nearby. Of course none of the MacLiven's people knew about the deal, so they assumed the child was the survivor of some other sinking, whereas Robbie didn't know what to think. Perhaps his child hadn't died after all, and the Germans had actually kept their side of the bargain. Or perhaps they'd simply snatched up some suitably aged kid at random in the knowledge that MacLiven couldn't recognize his own son anyway.'

I didn't say anything and after a moment she went on, 'Well, of course, there *wasn't* any way of knowing, but Robbie adopted the child just the same—adopted him and called him Charles.' She smiled faintly. 'I don't suppose he'd have much approved of Chas.'

No, I thought, I don't suppose he would, but that was the least of our worries. I said, 'And how much does Chas know about this?'

'Oh, Straun!' she said. 'Why do you think I was so keen to get rid of you? Don't you see I was scared stiff that you'd dig this up?' She drew a deep breath. 'Chas knows *nothing*! Except that he was washed up on the shore here and the laird looked after him and gave him a name. He takes it for granted that even if he wasn't a local he was at least Scots. Chas doesn't know and there's no reason why he ever should.'

'But if he did find out?'

'He could take his pick,' Kirstie said. 'Either he's the son of a man who was prepared to betray his country for the sake of his family or he's one hundred per cent German.'

I found myself thinking that there was nothing wrong in being one hundred per cent German but I could see it had less attraction if your way of life required you to be one hundred and ten per cent Scots. No wonder he had a weakness for tartan trews. Poor Chas. I said, 'Old Grant must have been talking in Gaelic for quite a time to tell you all this. Didn't your friends want a translation?'

Kirstie nodded. 'They did, as a matter of fact. I told them he was rambling on about the conversion of the islands.' She hesitated. 'But there's one thing that I don't understand—'

That made two of us, I thought, but I didn't want to discourage her. 'Yes?'

'How could Gavin Grant possibly know all this?'

I said, 'Because Robbie MacLiven told him.'

Kirstie blinked. 'But why, for goodness' sake?'

'Gavin Grant wasn't a pastor,' I told her. 'He was a Catholic priest. Robbie's priest. What he was telling you under the influence of that drug were the secrets of the confessional.'

CHAPTER 14

Rain was falling next morning, a thin mist that drifted in from the west, softening the light and putting sheen on the slate roof I could see from my bedroom window. So this was the Day of Wrath, I thought. I remembered the guests getting themselves organized for packed food, the checking of cameras for the right film. Odd how an ancient pagan ceremony could so easily become a tourist attraction. Sad, really. Like keeping a sabre-toothed tiger for a pet.

I put on slacks and a wool shirt, then, on impulse, pulled on a rainproof jacket. Everyone said that in Scotland one ignored the rain, so high time I did the same. In the mirror as I pulled up the zip I could see the paintings that had caught my eye the day I'd arrived and I went over and looked at them again. I knew nothing about abstracts, Laurie having said on more than one occasion that my taste in art was strictly G-Plan, the original chap who knew nothing except what he liked. Oh well.

The right-hand painting consisted largely of squares of different sizes, mainly black and white, overlaid with further squares that were offset. It was agreeable, in an odd way, but that was about all. It was signed 'R.M.' and when I took it down and looked at the back, a faded pencilled notation read 'Black Runner 1936'. If 'R.M.' was Robbie MacLiven and 1936 was the date of the Berlin Olympics, then the black runner could well have been Jesse Owens, but you could have fooled me.

I put the squares back and tried my luck with its companion piece. Standing back, I saw it was apparently another running figure, but more of a portrait. All lozenges of bright colour and seemingly unrelated shapes. I reached out and touched the surface, felt with my finger the craggy ridges of long-dried paint and wondered why it stirred some chord in me. I had a look, and on the back a scribble simply noted: *Katrina Running*.

So it was a portrait, all right. For the first time I sensed in my untutored way that perhaps after all a clever chap could capture something of a person without making a conventional likeness. I hung the painting on the wall again, an oddly satisfying thing that I could have lived with well enough. I found myself wishing that I knew enough about art to be able to tell if Robbie MacLiven's work had been any good or not. It hardly mattered now, but I couldn't help wondering whether it had been worth all the trouble.

Downstairs it seemed as though the rain was keeping people in bed because the breakfast-room was empty and apparently even the girl who looked after my table hadn't yet got her act together. Ailsa McCrae served me in person and with no very good grace.

'She's away with the rest of them at yon heathen gathering,' she said in answer to my question. 'Will you be having a round with himself later on?' Golf, apparently, was not heathen. Far from it.

I said, 'The MacLiven's not gone with the rest, then?'

Ailsa shook her head. 'He's no had his breakfast yet, but he said last night he hoped you'd have time for a hole or two.' She plucked at the sleeve of her cardigan to straighten it. 'If you're agreeable, that is.'

'That'll be fine,' I said. 'I'll look forward to it.'

She looked relieved, I thought. The faithful retainer, anxious that the young master should have his pleasure, no doubt. Or more likely, faithful retainer anxious to get him out of the way. 'If he's not down before I've finished breakfast,' I told her, 'I'll be in the library.'

He wasn't, so to the library I went. As a library it was no great shakes and Chas's design consultant had drawn pretty heavily on Hollywood, which, considering who was paying the bill, was probably excusable. I couldn't get along with a huge fibreglass globe but the chairs were comfortable and some of the glass-fronted shelving held real books. Most of the latter were modern but a small proportion must have come with the place. I looked for something on modern art but there was nothing much, so by the time Chas found me I'd skimmed through the few there were.

'Sorry, Angus, I didn't mean to keep you waiting, but you know the way it is.' Chas was still wearing his favourite tartan trews but otherwise he could have passed as a week-end golfer anywhere, although a shade green round the gills. Like most men with reddish hair, he didn't take kindly to the sun, and his years on the tournament circuit had left him with a complexion that was brick red. This morning the red was blotched and patchy and his customarily fierce blue eyes about half their usual size.

'Do you feel all right?' I suppose it would have been tactful to say nothing but there are some things one can't ignore.

Chas said shortly, 'I'm OK. Didn't sleep so good.' He nodded at the art books. 'What the hell are you doing reading that sort of crap this time of the morning?'

I said, 'I was trying to find something on the paintings of Robbie MacLiven.'

Chas grinned sourly. 'What makes you think my old man was good enough to get in the books?'

'Was he?'

'Hell, I shouldn't think so.' Chas frowned, as though struck by an original thought. 'I mean, have you *seen* any?'

'There are two in my room, for a start.'

Chas looked surprised, genuinely I thought. 'There are, at that. Black and white thing and something else, I forget what.'

I said, 'It's called "Katrina Running".'

'Is it now?' Chas shook his head. 'Never looked. You want to play a few holes?'

No, Chas, I do not want to play a few holes. I'd much rather ask you why you think Koch and Werner died, and why someone tried to electrocute Mr Mouse, but I can't because one thing will lead to another and I promised Kirstie. Which is a nonsense because any moment now a local copper is going to ask questions and he's not going to spare your feelings or anyone else's, come to that.

So in the end we let Rome burn and played a few holes, anyway.

The wind that had been carrying the fine rain had dropped and a pale sun was beginning to shine through, reflecting off the wet grass. A few seagulls sat around like paying spectators, waiting for the game to begin.

'Kind of quiet,' Chas said.

'I'm not complaining.' I pulled off my waterproof jacket and stowed it away in my bag. But he was right, it was so still you could hear the faint slop of the sea at the foot of the cliffs, and very little of that. With the guests and a good proportion of the staff busy gawping at the Ceilegh, the castle was as good as empty, which in my opinion was by no means a bad thing.

'Kind of nice having the place to ourselves,' Chas said.

It was an odd kind of morning. Golf is golf if you like the game well enough but there are limits to concentration when one has too much on one's mind. Still, we enjoyed ourselves in a mild kind of way and it was lunch-time and I was winning before I managed to lose a ball, hooking it decisively over the cliff. There wasn't much we could do except stand on the edge and have a cautious look.

'I can see it,' Chas said.

I could see it too, a tiny patch of white against the grey stone of the ledge on which it had lodged. It might well have been a bird's egg from where we stood, nestling cosily there with the blue sea lapping the rocks another hundred feet below.

'I can see it, too,' I said, 'but I don't intend doing anything about it.'

'My hole, your game.'

He was right but I was staring down at the drop below me. Behind me, Chas was saying, 'Come on, I'll buy you a drink.'

I said, 'Hang on a minute.' I don't know what it was: something to do with the height and the look of the thing, I suppose, but in my mind's eye I was looking down at the castle's underground passages and the chilling depths of the oubliette.

'Now what?' Chas was getting fretful.

'Look,' I told him, 'it sounds a daft question, but how did they actually *build* that oubliette?'

He stared at me, bright blue eyes squinting against the sun. 'They didn't build it, man, they dug it. Like a well.'

'It's faced,' I reminded him. 'Faced with granite blocks, bonded like brick.'

'So's a well.'

I said, 'You dig a well out with a spade and a bucket; no brickwork and the whole damn thing falls in on you. But that hellish dungeon of yours is built over a hole—you can hear the water down there. So whoever built it would have had to start at the bottom.'

Chas stared at me, swinging his 5 iron in his right hand as if he were a metronome. The idea was a new one but he was no fool. He said, 'For Chrissake, Angus, how? There's nothing under that cell thing for a man to stand on.'

'Like a hole that goes to the centre of the earth?'

'Well, no—'

'Have you ever been down there?'

'You know damn well I haven't.' Chas's voice had a touch of irritation. 'I haven't measured the earth to check that it's really round, either, but I'm prepared to take someone's word for that kind of thing.'

'Mind if we have a look?'

He thought for a moment. I don't think that he had any intention of saying 'No', but he was the kind of character who likes to know what he's agreeing to. Apparently the computer came up with the right response because he said, 'OK, go ahead. How do you plan to go about it?'

'There's that grille at the bottom,' I said. 'Have you got anything like a big torch?'

He nodded. 'Sure. Kind of portable flood thing I was planning to use outside the bar. There'll be a long cable lead in the workshop somewhere.'

'Better get a few tools while you're at it,' I told him. 'Cold chisels and a club hammer.'

'You fall through that hole, man, it's going to take one hell of a time to find you, let alone bring you up.'

'I'd just thought of that,' I said. 'Best if we get a rope, too.'

We found ourselves an assortment of gear and made our way downstairs. Ailsa McCrae was still in the kitchen making life difficult for some girl who was trying to load a dishwasher, and Chas begged an extending aluminium ladder from some secret store of maintenance equipment.

'You'll be letting me have that back, now. And clean.'

'I'll do that, Ailsa.' Chas might not be exactly his house-keeper's slave but the demarcation lines were a bit blurred at the edges.

'And ye'll no be breaking it.'

'No, ma'am.'

'Awa' wi' ye, then.'

Away we went. What with a couple of ladders, an assortment of fairly heavy tools and a massive Ayers Hyper Lite, there was a good deal of fetching and carrying to do, but we dropped the first of the ladders down to the floor of the oubliette and coupled up the lamp. The bulb came alight with an audible pop and I winced in the halogen glare, suppressing an urge to warm my hands on the thing because down at the bottom of The Hole it was as cold and damp as it had been the first time.

Chas was saying, 'Jesus, what a place!' and I couldn't find anything to improve on that. I'd been hoping that the atmosphere down at the bottom might not be quite as bad a second time around but, if anything, it was worse. I found myself wondering what sort of man would have been able to cope with the cold and the loneliness and the dark without going mad. Perhaps none did. Perhaps they all went crazy and beat their brains out against these rough granite walls. I glanced at Chas and saw that his face was shining with sweat. It might be his castle but apparently there were bits of it that got to him, too.

'Give me a hand to hold this thing,' I said, because the Hyper Lite was heavy. Chas shuffled over and clamped his big hands round the base and together we pointed the beam downwards through the grille in the floor.

'Pretty, ain't it?' Chas said.

There was sea down there, fifteen feet or so below us, the water we could hear in the oubliette. The white beam of torchlight showed it surging steadily past, presumably because the tide pushed in through some opening and was sucked away by way of some tortuous route deep below the island. I was reminded of the underground rivers I'd seen on my one potholing expedition, an experience yes, but not one to be repeated. I shone the light sideways and caught a glimpse of a platform of rock, too regular to be natural.

I said, 'Let's get this grille out.'

It was easy enough to say. Chas had brought an eighteen-inch cold chisel with him and we took it in turns to bash at the age-old mortar that held the iron grid in place. It was cold as charity down there but by the time we'd finished we were sweating. We lifted it free and the sound of the sea seemed to come up to us clearer, though that must have been an illusion because a few bars could hardly have made that difference.

'Is the MacLiven there?'

I looked over my shoulder and up to the entrance to The Hole. The trapdoor was open and Miss McCrae was peering down, much as the gaoler must have looked down on his charge in the old days.

Chas said, 'Aye.' I wondered if it was the place that was getting to him or if he was making an effort to speak like everybody else, but either way, the result raised the hairs on the back of one's neck. The accent was too good for comfort.

'There's—' Chas's housekeeper paused and apparently decided that a visitor was a visitor. 'There's two gentlemen to see you.'

'Holy cow!' Chas said. 'Now?'

A voice said, 'Yes, now.' There was a momentary shadow as figures filled the entrance, the ladder creaked and two people came down backwards. After a moment's hesitation Ailsa followed them.

She said in an aggrieved tone, 'I told them you were busy. They pushed their way in.'

'God save all here,' said Sean Donovan.

CHAPTER 15

I straightened my back and looked up at the Heavenly Twins. Not for nothing the concept of a comely Lucifer. If the Donovan brothers had been hairy, shambling sub-humans, one would have faced them with a certain equa-nimity, but in fact they were an extraordinarily good-looking pair. The Daves and Basils of the Crofter Community might be an unpleasant lot but, with their weird looks, more sad than scary. Not so Sean and Patrick. On a wet night in Ireland they probably looked like just two more raincoated tearaways, but here it was different, where leather shirts and bits of snakeskin round their foreheads turned them into a cross between Tarzan and Rambo. Comic strip stuff until you looked into those crazed eyes and realized what you were up against. These people were following no fuzzy star of a freeloading world, they knew exactly what they were doing. These were IRA hard men who'd blow a pubload of strangers into strips of raw meat just to try out a new timing device. Trained terrorists, latter day Ninja, who'd kill almost by reflex anyone who stood in their way.

'You want something?' Chas was making an effort to sound overjoyed at their arrival.

'We'll just be looking down there.' Sean pointed to the black square where the grille had been. He limped on a bandaged foot but seemed to be managing all right, which was a pity.

Chas either didn't notice the warning sign or didn't care, because he picked up the cold chisel and swung it in his big hand. 'Motherloving freak, get the hell out of here or I'll beat the shit outta you.' Chas, off colour, lacked finesse.

'It's your girl we're holding back there,' Sean said.

There was a silence, broken only by the slop of water below us. Sean said with a kind of patience, 'We're after holding Kirstie Stewart. With the Crofters, at Ardrossan.'

There was a silence at the bottom of the oubliette, and in it I tried to remember when I'd seen her last. It wasn't an exercise that gave me much comfort because I realized that Kirstie hadn't been around all morning.

Patrick seemed to read my mind without difficulty. 'She came with the others for the Ceilegh, so she did. Dave will be asking her to stay.'

Most policemen have moments when they would welcome a world without journalists and their insatiable curiosity. Kirstie must have been out of her mind going back to the commune, banking on her ordinary dress to be an effective disguise. I thought uncharitably that, like all reporters, she'd dived head first into trouble and now, true to form, she'd expect us to get her out.

Chas said thickly, 'You stupid bastards, she went with a load of people from this hotel. You think you can snatch her in broad daylight just like that?'

'Now isn't it a fact that they all went to see a lot of people who should know better staring at the sun an' waiting for something to happen?' Sean asked him. He made a gesture of impatience. 'They'll not notice anything, so hurry along and show us what it is you've got down there and you'll have no need to worry.'

'And if I don't?'

Patrick said bleakly, 'Listen, Yank, if we're not back by five o'clock with the good news, the girl's going to be shot so full of heroin you'll *never* get her back.'

I didn't want to tell Chas, but I'd seen the odd lost soul who'd been forcibly pumped full of heroin, a kind of spiritual kneecapping. You didn't have to become an addict afterwards but the detoxification was much the same as if you'd been on the stuff for years. I said to Chas, 'Do as he says.'

'But—'

I didn't argue, I just took the ladder and dropped it through the floor of the cell. Nobody made any move so after a moment I went down it myself. Not unreasonable, since I was the one who had the torch. It was only about ten steps but it seemed a lot more than that before my feet touched the ledge we'd seen from above. I gave the electric cable a jerk to get down some of the slack and flashed the Hyper Lite around.

It was potholing again with a vengeance. If I'd never

spent that cold and terrifying weekend in the Mendips, what I was looking at would have come as something of a shock; as it was, the whole thing was not unfamiliar. I was standing in a vaulted cavern through which water flowed in a surging, oily stream from right to left, gurgling and splashing its way between jagged rock walls that reflected seaweed green in the lamp's white beam. From where the sea came there was a faint patch of light, which I guessed to be what little there was of a dry entry to the cave, and to the left the black water vanished into a tunnel that presumably found its way back to the sea. The place was cold, and frightening, and full of a low, continuous roar.

From above me, Sean's voice called impatiently, 'Let's be having some light, then!'

I flipped the lamp upwards and watched the others come down. It looked exactly as though they were descending from some kind of giant wasps' nest, because the ancient workmen had built the oubliette from the outside, with only about a quarter of its circumference consisting of the rock wall. I remembered once seeing a cliff fall somewhere in Norfolk where the earth had slipped away to reveal part of a brick-lined well, and it had looked exactly the same.

We stood in silence for a moment, and I swung the light about so the others could take it all in. Even the Heavenly Twins were unexpectedly silent and it was Chas who stamped his foot on the broad shelf on which we were standing and said with a kind of awe, 'For God's sake, Angus! It's man made!'

It was as man made as a London bus. I shone the lamp down on the square stone blocks. It was hard to see the straight quarryman's lines between them because of weed and a million tiny crustaceans that had made their home there, but nature certainly hadn't contributed anything to it other than the raw materials. 'It's a quay,' I said. There was no means of guessing who had made it or when. Some

long-dead MacLiven with an eye to avoiding Excise men?
For all I knew, even further back, when clan raided clan
and a defensible mooring would have been a priceless asset
to an island fortress. I traced the lamp beam along the side
that dropped sheer to the water six feet below. There
was even a granite stump that must have been set in as a
bollard.

'An old quay,' Sean said suddenly. Then, as the penny
dropped, '*The* old quay!'

I said, 'Yes, this is the one Gavin Grant meant. You've
been diving off the wrong one.'

I heard Chas make some sort of strangled sound of protest
but it was too late to duck around the truth any more. I
swung the cold arc of the lamp towards the faint blur of
light where the sea came in, and it picked out a disorganized
rubble of rock, piece piled on piece like the remains of some
demolished church. I said, 'That used to be the way in.
They'd have unloaded supplies straight on to the quay here
and then hauled them up into the castle.' I found myself
thinking that, with secrecy and security such as this, early
MacLivens might well have tried their hands at a little
modest piracy from time to time—certainly the place would
have been ideal.

Chas said in a choking voice, 'Will someone tell me what
the hell this is all about?'

Well, he was going to have to know sooner or later. I
knew that Kirstie wouldn't thank me for it but then, Kirstie
wasn't here and, in any case, she should have told him long
ago.

'Sure an' I'll tell you.' Sean Donovan made the decision
for me. 'Your old man had no more time for the bloody
British than I have, did you know that? A German naval
boat called in here during the war because her commander
knew he'd be sure of a welcome—'

Chas wasn't looking at him, instead he was staring in my

direction as though I was the one who knew whether or not it was true.

'It was one hell of a welcome,' I said. 'Robbie MacLiven blew him out of the water for his pains.'

It must have made quite a bang in such a confined space. I had to imagine the explosion but not the rest, because I knew that, on the authority of the only witness still alive.

'*Only a couple of frames on this film,*' Mr Mouse had said. And when I'd printed that picture of poor Luther falling through space, I'd noticed the same thing. Or thought I did. Only in the odd way that minds have, mine had settled on a flaw in that statement and wouldn't leave it alone. Luther Koch's fall had been on frames numbered 19, 20 and 21 instead of 1, 2 and 3, and I kept asking myself how a photographer of Meuse's standing could have managed to wreck those eighteen preceding ones. But *had* he wrecked them? Develop a blank frame and it comes up clear, whereas frames 1 to 18 had been grey, which meant that they had at least been exposed. But with what? There appeared to be no detail, so what had been photographed? A wall? Sheets of paper? I'd gone back to the darkroom and blown them up on the enlarger, one by one.

And that's exactly what they were—sheets of paper, because Max Meuse had been busy before he left Israel. And no wonder he'd loaded his camera with monochrome; he'd photographed the record of the questioning of Carl Roschmann. Page after page of it, in Hebrew, with a side-by-side translation in English and German. It wasn't a complete story, because Roschmann's memory simply hadn't been able to come up with all the answers, but there was enough for even bits and pieces read at random to make his story come alive.

PRESIDENT: You say you arrived off the coast of

	Scotland safely. Can you describe the port where you berthed?
ROSCHMANN:	No, sir. I can only remember there was a quay. A very small quay.
PRESIDENT:	Was there anyone about?
ROSCHMANN:	Only one man, who had been waiting for us. A Scotsman. I remember him because he was the first man I'd ever seen who wore a kilt. He shouted to Commander Ritter that the fuel was ready and that he was welcome to stay until it got dark.
PRESIDENT:	Did he speak in German?
ROSCHMANN:	Yes, I remember his German was quite good. Accented but fluent.
PRESIDENT:	Do you remember what happened next?
ROSCHMANN:	Yes, sir. The Scotsman said to Commander Ritter, 'I have kept my side of the bargain, now it is your turn to keep yours. Where is my son?' The Commander replied that he was below and he sent Petty Officer Neumann to bring him up.
PRESIDENT:	Were you surprised to hear the Scotsman refer to his son?
ROSCHMANN:	Very surprised. We—the crew members, that is—had imagined the child belonged to some important Party official. But the Commander ordered Neumann to give him to the Scotsman, who took him in his arms.
PRESIDENT:	How old would you say the child was?

ROSCHMANN:	I know little of children, but I should think about three.
PRESIDENT:	Go on.
ROSCHMANN:	Commander Ritter suggested to the Scotsman that, as it would not be dark for some hours, he might care to invite our officers ashore for a drink and the hospitality of his castle.
PRESIDENT:	He said 'castle'?
ROSCHMANN:	Yes, I remember because I was surprised at the time.
PRESIDENT:	And did the Scotsman agree?
ROSCHMANN:	No, sir. He became angry and said something about being particular about the people he invited to his home. Our other officer, Lieutenant Schmidt, took offence at that and shouted that in that case the Scotsman might as well drop the child in the sea because far from being his own son, he was just a brat picked out of an orphanage.
PRESIDENT:	What did the Scotsman say to that?
ROSCHMANN:	I thought for a moment he was going to try to hand the child back, but he only said, 'So you broke your word. I was rather expecting that.' Then he turned and went to the back of the quay. I can't quite remember. I think he went up some steps. We just stood there waiting until all at once there was a tremendous explosion and our vessel seemed to fly apart . . .

The explosion would have brought down the entrance to the hidden quay, so that nothing would get in there again. And most certainly nothing that was already there would ever get out.

'Well, let's be looking for the wreck, then.' Sean was looking down over the edge of the quay. He was a single-minded soul.

I flashed the light towards the entrance to the tunnel down which the sea was emptying itself. 'Over there, I imagine. What little there's left.' Jammed against the wall were a few spars and formers of twisted metal. Forty years of the Atlantic current hadn't left very much. Whatever treasures had been loaded on the MTB had long ago been sucked away and spread over the sea bed and out into the Atlantic. Gone like the paymaster's gold of the Armada, never to return.

'Holy Mary!' The brothers moved forward and I watched them without sympathy. A lot of work and little to show for it, but what was Chas thinking? I turned and saw that he too was standing on the edge of the quay, staring towards what was left of the wreck. He was breathing heavily and his face looked dreadful. Suddenly, and for no reason, Ailsa McCrae ran towards him. She ran with her left arm stretching out, reaching for him, and in that moment I not only knew for certain who she was but also what she'd done. That shadowy figure against the fog in Mr Meuse's photograph of Luther Koch's death fall had its left arm stretched out in just the same way. So did the woman in the painting that hung in my room. It had been Ailsa McCrae who had pushed Luther Koch off that cliff. Ailsa McCrae who had been the subject of Robbie MacLiven's painting all those years ago.

I shouted, 'Katrina!' and ran. It wasn't far to go and I had her by the arm before she had a chance to shove Chas into the torrent. She struggled wildly for a moment, fighting with incredible strength for an old woman. Chas stayed where he was with his back to us, and I wondered how he could possibly not have heard us. But then he turned unhurriedly and I saw that his eyes were staring beyond me at God knows what.

'It's coming!' he said, and his voice was thick and slurred as though he was drunk. 'Get the hell out of here, I tell you! The *Fearg*'s coming!' Still without seeing me, he began to run towards the ladder in a curious, stumbling gait. I heard the aluminium rungs rattle behind me as he climbed and I still struggled with the maniac strength of Ailsa McCrae.

She collapsed all at once and I stood there holding her, breathing hard. What in God's name had come over Chas? I wondered. The water was flowing quietly past us as before, nothing seemed to have changed. *The Fearg is coming*. The Wrath. What Wrath was coming?

I looked down at the woman I was holding. 'Come on, Katrina,' I said. 'We'd better get out of here.'

I led her to the ladder but she seemed reluctant to climb it, so I went first, one hand round her wrist, tugging her gently after me. She followed slowly and then, as I looked back at her, I saw the water rise. It was quite the most terrifying thing I'd seen in my life. There was no wave, but the sea simply rose up, presumably driven by some extraordinary freak underwater current. It swept up in seconds to the level of the quay and then just as quickly beyond it. I saw it surge over the place where we'd been standing minutes before in a bewildering unstoppable wall of sea, three feet deep, that swept the Heavenly Twins off their feet before they knew what was happening and sucked them down and into the roaring tumult at the exit cave. The surge crashed against the bottom of the steps as I leapt upwards towards the bottom of the oubliette where the trapdoor awaited me.

I reached it and scrambled through, turned and grabbed Ailsa McCrae by a wrist just as the water came up to meet me. It swept over her, dragging her feet off the ladder. For a moment I hung on but she was being pulled by something that was more than human. Suddenly I wasn't holding her wrist any more and the last thing I saw of her was the number they had tattooed on her arm in Auschwitz concentration camp more than forty years ago.

CHAPTER 16

I didn't have much time to mourn her because the water welled up through the hole we'd made in the bottom of the oubliette and lifted me like a cork in a bottle. If there'd been a lot of roaring and foaming, it would have been terrifying enough but less chilling than the menace of this silent onrush of water which made one feel like something caught in the bottom of a lock.

Someone bumped into me and I saw it was Chas. I saw him grab the bottom of the ladder and start to haul himself up it, but next moment the water surged up and overtook him, lifting him off the slippery aluminium treads so that the two of us were floundering about together like unfortunate cats who'd fallen into a well. By this time I'd succeeded in dropping the lamp, which through some triumph of waterproofing continued to operate ten feet below the surface, effectively lighting the water in the cell with a rather stagey phosphorescent green glow.

'Easy,' I said, 'let it take us up.' The competent police officer should by his example restrain any tendency towards panic.

Chas shook his head free of water like a dog and I saw that there was blood running down from beneath his hair and I realized he must have hurt himself coming off the ladder. He asked thickly, 'Where's Ailsa?'

It wasn't a question that needed answering, which Chas must have realized because he didn't ask again. The water went on rising and I bent my head back so that I could see the open trapdoor above us, and concentrated on it hard, because that way I didn't have to think what it would have been like to be a prisoner when this happened, down there in the dark with the trap bolted shut. Forget it, I thought, that was a hell of a long time ago.

I trod water and saw that the ladder hadn't been shifted by the inrush of water so I pushed Chas towards it because, although by now the trap was only three feet or so above us, it was still too high to make a grab for the edge.

'Get up!' I shouted at him. 'Up and out, quick!' I'd noticed that the water-level was almost up to the grated openings high up in the walls of the cell and I didn't fancy having him pinned against them when the water started to rush through. I think he'd worked that one out for himself, because he grabbed the steps and hung on to them once more as though his life depended on it, which in fact it probably did. He turned to me and his ugly face made the grimace that served him as a grin, and he said in what Americans fondly suppose to be upper-class English, 'After you, old boy. Captain's the last to leave the ship.'

There are times when it's best not to argue. I grabbed a rung and wrenched myself free of the water, three steps and I had my arms through the trap and flat on the floor above. I wriggled out and rolled free as Chas's head appeared behind me. He was prepared to stay with the sinking ship but I was glad to see that he showed no intention of going down with it.

'Jeeesus!' He hauled himself out and flopped down beside me, staring back through the square in the floor at the surface of the water slurping within touch distance. It must have risen from the bottom of the oubliette to the top in no more than thirty seconds. Chas looked at me as it struck him that at its present rate of progress it was only going to need another half-minute to have the sea through the trap and into the bar upstairs. He muttered, 'D'you think—'

I shook my head. 'No, it's as high now as it'll go.' I pointed downwards. Those grilles at the top of the oubliette had puzzled me when I'd first seen them because they'd seemed odd places to have windows. But, of course, they weren't windows. 'They're spillways,' I said. 'When the tide reaches them it just overflows through the grille. A sort of built-in fail-safe device.'

'You're kidding.'

'Then watch it.'

We watched it together. The surface of the water reached the grilles, hung there for a moment by surface tension, then burst through in a torrent of yeasty foam.

I said, 'Whoever built that cell knew about the Rage all right.'

'Yes.' Chas was staring down at the water and, even as he watched, it fell back from the grilles. A moment later it had fallen an inch. Two. Four.

'Show's over,' I said. The Heavenly Twins were down below us somewhere, those beautiful bodies tumbling over and over in some submarine cave. Ailsa McCrae was down there, too, but I didn't want to think about her too much. Well, the show was over all right, though I didn't have to put it quite like that.

'I knew,' Chas said, 'I tell you, man, I *knew*!'

'I knew it was coming,' Chas was saying to Kirstie. We were in his flat above the bar and all was well with her. Scared stiff, which in the long run might prove to be a good thing, suitably chastened by Chas's laying down of the law.

'You get into one more fix like that, Princess, and you get yourself out! You hear me?'

She'd heard him all right. Lucky for Chas that she hadn't seen him in the chopper, worried cross-eyed about getting to the Crofters in time, and hating my guts for insisting that we picked up Constable Macdonald first.

'You're supposed to be a goddam cop, aren't you? What d'you want help for? *I'll* help you if you're worried about those freaks—'

'It's his patch,' I'd told him. 'We've also seen three people drowned. It may not look like it, but we *need* Macdonald.' The truth was *I* needed Macdonald, not being all that sure I could restrain Chas on my own and not wanting half a dozen slain Crofters on my hands. In the end it had turned out all right, Kirstie frightened but unharmed, Chas muttering but no blood, and Constable Macdonald grim and taking names.

But now, listening to the two of them, I realized that Chas wasn't making it up. It was true, he really had known that terrifying surge of water was coming. I remembered the look in his eyes down there as he'd shouted the warning. No wonder he'd looked odd all day, half of him knowing that something extraordinary was going to happen, the rational half trying to convince him that it was not.

'It's the Sight, darling,' Kirstie told him gently. 'The Eye of the MacLiven, or whatever it is they call it. Don't you remember? You lot have had it since Day One.'

Chas looked at her. 'Right! So why me? Robbie MacLiven picked me out of the sea—remember? Sure he took me as his son, but whatever blood's in my veins, it's not his, so how in hell do I come to inherit the Sight?'

Kirstie put her arms round him. 'You're the long lost prince, love. For God's sake, what does it matter?' She did not look at me.

Chas stroked her shoulder absently. At that moment, and

I suppose at any moment, the age bit didn't matter. He said slowly, 'Can't you understand, girl? I *want* to be a MacLiven. But I got to know how.'

'I'll tell you how,' I said. I ignored the anguished expression on Kirstie's face. 'What you don't appreciate is the pressure the Nazis put on your father in order to get alongside the old quay.'

I paused to let the 'your father' bit sink in. Then I went on, 'You know Robbie MacLiven lived in Germany before the war. What you don't know is that he met your mother there.'

Chas blinked. 'You mean he was married?'

'I don't honestly know,' I confessed, 'but whether he was married or not, he had a child—a son—by a girl he called Katrina.'

Chas said slowly, 'That's a Scots name.'

'Yes,' I agreed. 'She could have been a Scot. Or her name might have been the German version—Katherina—and Robbie chose to call her Katrina because it was more familiar. Does it matter?'

'I guess not,' Chas said. 'What happened to her?'

'The war happened,' I said. 'Just before the balloon went up Robbie came home in a hurry. He only just made it. Katrina was in another part of the country at the time and in spite of his efforts he couldn't find her, so in the end he came back to Scotland leaving the girl and her child behind. He used every contact he knew to get in touch with her, but it was no use. All he could discover was that she had joined one of the student anti-fascist resistance movements, been arrested and sent to a concentration camp. There, both she and the child were reported to have died.

'God knows what Robbie MacLiven felt when he heard about that but it couldn't have cheered him up much. Whatever sympathy he may once have had for the German people certainly wouldn't have survived that bit of news, and there wasn't a soul with whom he could share his sorrow. Then in 1943 he was approached by someone acting on behalf of a member of the Nazi inner ring, asking him to provide a haven for an MTB. On the face of it the request was absurd—your father may have owned an ideal site for such an operation but he was also the last man likely to agree to such a suggestion. But as it happened, the Nazis held a winning card.' I paused.

Chas said tentatively, 'Me?'

I nodded. 'Yes, you. I don't know how the Nazis discovered that Robbie was your father—probably the Gestapo got that out of some unfortunate resistance prisoner. But it was a sound reason for keeping you alive against a time when such a bargaining ploy might prove useful.'

'And they were right.'

'Of course. They told your father that although the mother was dead, the child was alive and well. If he would just shelter a small boat and its crew for a few hours they would pay for the facilities by returning his son.'

I saw the expression on Chas's face. 'Look,' I said, 'it was one hell of a temptation. Robbie was already a sick man who probably guessed he hadn't many more years to live and he desperately wanted—needed—his son. Moreover, it had been made clear to him that the service he was being asked to perform would be of no military assistance to his country's enemies. If he carried it out he would not cause the death of a single Allied serviceman, nor would it prolong the war by a single day. I don't know what you or I would have done in his position but luckily it's not a decision we've ever had to make. But back in 1943 Robbie weighed it all up and in the end he agreed with the Germans that they had a deal.'

'I'm surprised he believed the bastards,' Chas said.

'I don't think he did,' I told him. 'Over the centuries I imagine there's been a fair amount of sharp practice between

the highland clans—you've only got to read your history to
realize that every glen has its record of double-dealing and
treachery. Robbie MacLiven was nobody's fool and he
wasn't going into any deal without covering himself, so just
in case his visitors tried to double-cross him, he mined the
old quay and wired the whole thing so that he'd have the
red button where it would be most handy.

'As it turned out, the Germans really did arrive with a
small boy and what's more, they handed him over alive and
kicking. I suspect that was something of a surprise, but after
Robbie had taken the child from the Germans there was an
exchange of words between them. One of the German
officers was tempted to suggest that the small boy wasn't
really MacLiven's son—he was simply the first kid of the
appropriate age that could be found in a German orphanage.
God knows, the officer said, *what* nationality the boy was.
He might be anything from a German to a Jew. But most
certainly he wasn't a Scot.

'Angry he may have been, but it was a daft thing to say.
Whether or not Robbie realized later that he'd needled the
man is something we'll never know, but at the time it
convinced him that he'd been tricked. He bade the Germans
a formal goodbye, marched up the steps that in those days
led down to the old quay and smacked down the button.
There was one hell of a bang and that was that. Of course,
Robbie never did get to know the truth but I think in his
heart he believed what the officer had said—that his real
son was dead and that he'd had some orphan German
foisted on him. That was why he sent you off to the States.
He'd adopted you and brought you up as his own flesh and
blood, but I imagine he was happier if you weren't around
all the time just to make him wonder. But old Robbie
misjudged the Germans. They'd played fair with him after
all, and the proof's the fact that you've got the Sight.'

For a long time Chas just sat and looked at the whisky

in his glass. He didn't even raise his eyes when he asked, 'OK, Angus, how do you happen to know all this?'

'Kirstie will tell you some time.' I could rely on her to make sure that Father Grant never knew.

Chas looked at her. 'Will you?'

'Yes, darling. If you really want to know.'

He stood up then, looking at me for the first time. 'Thanks, Angus. I think I'll take me a walk for a while.'

Kirstie and I watched him go. 'Stop sniffing,' I told her.

She said, 'I'm not sniffing,' but she blew her nose just the same. Then she looked at me accusingly, 'Was Ailsa McCrae Chas's mother?'

'Yes.'

'Why didn't you tell Chas?'

I said, 'Because it's better he doesn't know. Sooner or later he might put two and two together and work out for himself that it was Mum who pushed Werner into the oubliette just as she shoved Luther Koch over the cliff. She wired poor old Meuse up to the mains and damn nearly knocked him off because she guessed he'd photographed her in the act, and if I hadn't been there to stop her, she'd have had her own son into the drink only half an hour ago.'

'But why Chas?' Kirstie asked. 'And why Werner, for that matter? He was Afrikaans.'

'So far as she was concerned, Chas was still the small boy some unknown Nazi had sent from Germany,' I told her. 'Poor Werner was just a mistake—his name and accent threw her. I remember how surprised she was when we went through his wallet and found out he came from South Africa.' I stopped. It's always difficult to try to justify a murder, and I wasn't sure whether I was doing that or not. 'She really did spend the war in a camp and I suppose she had an appalling time and ended up with a compulsion to knock off any German who strayed into her home ground. Every man his own invasion. She was insane, of course.'

'She may have been insane,' Kirstie said, 'but who *was* she?'

'Quite honestly,' I told her, 'I don't know. I was only sure that Ailsa and Katrina were the same person when the penny dropped and I realized that the abstract in my room was recognizably Ailsa McCrae.'

'So *nobody* knows who she really was.'

I smiled. 'Gavin Grant probably does, but he's not telling. I paid a call on him this morning after I'd finished making my report. All he'd say was that she was a Scots girl who'd been a student at Heidelberg when she met Robbie. After the war she made her way back here, hoping to find him. She'd lost all her relatives, and it fell to Grant to tell her that the laird was dead too, and the castle shut up. He got her the job as caretaker cum housekeeper, and of course when Chas finally arrived she didn't recognize him as her son. Not after all that time. In fact she was convinced that her son was dead and Chas was an impostor until those last moments when she realized that he really had got the MacLiven Sight.'

Kirstie was silent for a long time. Finally she asked: 'What do you suppose poor Gavin Grant will do now?'

'I gather there's a religious order not far from here that he has an interest in,' I told her. 'Not exactly a monastery, more of a retreat. Anyway, he's made up his mind to settle there, and he's giving the house and land back to the MacLivens—to Chas.'

'And the Crofters?'

A good question. I said, 'I suspect Chas won't be quite as indulgent. The travelling folk will soon be travelling again.'

We sat around a while longer. I asked her when she was going to marry Chas and she said soon. Then she asked me when I was planning to leave and I said tomorrow. After that Chas came back and I went off and left them together.

*

It was late in the evening two days later when I got back to London. A light rain was falling, people were busy knocking into each other with umbrellas and you couldn't get a taxi because their drivers had all gone home to watch a football match on the tele. After trying four pay-phones I managed to find one that hadn't been vandalized and rang Laurie.

'How was the golf?'

'Fair to middling,' I said.

'I presume that means you lost.'

'As a matter of fact I didn't finish my match.'

'What happened? Your opponent drop dead?'

'Something like that. Laurie, my love, we can do better than this,' I said. 'I've missed you.'

'You're a bastard, Angus,' the phone told me. 'I suppose you'd better come round.'

'Coming,' I said. I put the phone back and a woman with a lot of plastic shopping-bags put three of them down and reached for it gratefully. At least I'd pleased someone. Outside the station the rain had stopped. With any luck the football had been cancelled and then the taxis would come out too.

THE END